ELMORE LEONARD

Picket Line and Other Stories

PENGUIN BOOKS

PENGUIN CLASSICS

UK | USA | Canada | Ireland | Australia
India | New Zealand | South Africa

Penguin Classics is part of the Penguin Random House group of companies whose addresses can be found at global.penguinrandomhouse.com.

Penguin Random House UK
One Embassy Gardens, 8 Viaduct Gardens, London SW11 7BW

penguin.co.uk

'Picket Line' is an archival text, written as part of a project that did not come to fruition and is previously unpublished. 'Chick Killer' was published in *McSweeney's* in 2011. 'Ice Man' was published in *The Atlantic* in 2012.

First published in Penguin Classics 2025
001

Copyright © the Estate of Elmore Leonard, 2025

Penguin Random House values and supports copyright.
Copyright fuels creativity, encourages diverse voices, promotes freedom of expression and supports a vibrant culture. Thank you for purchasing an authorized edition of this book and for respecting intellectual property laws by not reproducing, scanning or distributing any part of it by any means without permission. You are supporting authors and enabling Penguin Random House to continue to publish books for everyone.
No part of this book may be used or reproduced in any manner for the purpose of training artificial intelligence technologies or systems. In accordance with Article 4(3) of the DSM Directive 2019/790, Penguin Random House expressly reserves this work from the text and data mining exception.

Set in 11.25/14pt Dante MT Std
Typeset by Six Red Marbles UK, Thetford, Norfolk
Printed and bound in Great Britain by Clays Ltd, Elcograf S.p.A.

The authorized representative in the EEA is Penguin Random House Ireland, Morrison Chambers, 32 Nassau Street, Dublin D02 YH68

A CIP catalogue record for this book is available from the British Library

ISBN: 978-0-241-75539-6

Penguin Random House is committed to a sustainable future for our business, our readers and our planet. This book is made from Forest Stewardship Council® certified paper.

PENGUIN MODERN CLASSICS: CRIME AND ESPIONAGE

Picket Line and Other Stories

1. Davis Grubb: NIGHT OF THE HUNTER
2. Edogawa Rampo: BEAST IN THE SHADOWS
3. Dorothy B. Hughes: IN A LONELY PLACE
4. Josephine Tey: THE FRANCHISE AFFAIR
5. Eric Ambler: JOURNEY INTO FEAR
6. John le Carré: CALL FOR THE DEAD
7. Georges Simenon: MAIGRET AND THE HEADLESS CORPSE
8. Len Deighton: SS-GB
9. Ross Macdonald: THE DROWNING POOL
10. Chester Himes: COTTON COMES TO HARLEM
11. Dick Lochte: SLEEPING DOG
12. Raymond Chandler: THE BIG SLEEP and FAREWELL, MY LOVELY
13. Anthony Price: OTHER PATHS TO GLORY
14. Edogawa Rampo: THE BLACK LIZARD
15. Michael Gilbert: GAME WITHOUT RULES
16. Georges Simenon: MAIGRET'S REVOLVER
17. C. S. Forester: PAYMENT DEFERRED
18. Eric Ambler: THE MASK OF DIMITRIOS
19. Josephine Tey: BRAT FARRAR
20. John le Carré: TINKER TAILOR SOLDIER SPY
21. Ross Macdonald: THE UNDERGROUND MAN
22. John Franklin: THE DEADLY PERCHERON
23. Robert Van Gulik: THE CHINESE GOLD MURDERS
24. Cornell Woolrich: I MARRIED A DEAD MAN
25. Ian Fleming: FROM RUSSIA WITH LOVE
26. Anthony Price: THE LABYRINTH MAKERS
27. John le Carré: THE NIGHT MANAGER
28. Edogawa Rampo: GOLD MASK
29. Georges Simenon: NIGHT AT THE CROSSROADS
30. Shirley Jackson: WE HAVE ALWAYS LIVED IN THE CASTLE
31. Elmore Leonard: THE SWITCH
32. Elmore Leonard: SWAG
33. Elmore Leonard: RUM PUNCH
34. Elmore Leonard: PICKET LINE AND OTHER STORIES

35. Elmore Leonard: 52 PICKUP
36. Elmore Leonard: CITY PRIMEVAL
37. Elmore Leonard: CAT CHASER

Picket Line and Other Stories

Contents

Picket Line   1
Chick Killer   79
Ice Man   87

Picket Line

1.

Chino had been driving since Eagle Pass, down 83 through Laredo, down through the vacant land of dust-green mesquite and sunglare and bugs rising with the airstream over the hood and exploding in yellow bursts against the windshield. Like somebody was spitting them there.

Paco Rojas said, 'Man, I'm in pain.'

Chino was counting the bug stains, more than a dozen of the yellow ones: some kind of bug flying along having a nice time and the next moment sucked into the wind, coming fast up over the hood and wiped out, the bug not kowing what in the name of Christ happened to him. Maybe they had been butterflies. Seeing the bugs suddenly, there wasn't time to tell what they were. Chino looked at the speedometer and up again, touching his sunglasses at the bridge. He was holding between 80 and 85 down the two-lane highway that rose and dropped through the emptiness-brush hiding the river somewhere off to the right – passing no signs, no cars, no people, only, every few miles, silver litter barrels that were lined with plastic bags.

'You hear me? I got to piss.'

Paco Rojas, in the back seat, had slept since Eagle Pass, stretched out belly up, mouth open, eyes hidden beneath thick sagging brows, a face that had been hit often and turned to leather, an ex-welterweight body turning light-heavy. When he sat up he hunched over to rest his arms on the front seat and stare through the windshield.

'All you got to do is stop the car.'

'We need gas,' Chino said. 'I'm not going to stop twice.'

'How long you think it take me, an hour? Man, I got to go *now*.'

Maybe they were all different kinds of bugs, but all bugs were yellow inside. Like all people were red inside. Maybe. He'd never thought about it before. Chino's gaze held on the stained windshield as he waited for a bug to come over the hood.

2.

The Texaco station attendant wore a dark green shirt with the name *Gil* stitched over the pocket. He was big for a Mexican, or a Mexican-American or a Chicano or a Latin or whatever a dark-skinned man with a little mustache might be called in this town in the Lower Rio Grande Valley. Benson, Pop. 1320. Reduce Speed to 40. Though if a car went through at 80 there would be nothing on the street to hit. The station attendant was inside, breaking open a roll of quarters and letting them slide into the cash register. When the bell rang and he saw the Mercury – brown one, a couple of years old – rolling up to the pumps, he called out, 'I got it.' The sound of a pneumatic wrench, coming from the attached service area, stopped and then started again.

The car was a mess. It had been traveling at least two three days, yes, California plates, a couple of guys getting out he had never seen before. Chicanos. That surprised him. But not migrants. Sport shirts, nice pants kind of tight and low on their hips, nice shoes, or boots they looked like. The one with the sunglasses stood looking around with his hands on his hips. The other one, tough-looking guy, said, 'Where you take a leak at?', coming toward the station, passing the attendant and not waiting. The attendant pointed and said over his shoulder, 'Around the side. The key's in the office, on a board.' Then to the other one, nice-looking guy in the yellow sport shirt and sunglasses, he said, 'Fill it up?'

Chino nodded, not looking at the attendant but at the station. 'You got any beer?'

'Up the street,' the attendant said. 'Place has a sign, Hi-Life.'

Chino thought about it, staring at the deserted highway through town, at the frame and adobe storefronts and rusting signs. There were telephone poles in a line down the street but no sign of trees. Beyond the buildings, across the sweep of brush country to the horizon, there were no tall stands of trees. Chino walked over to the station and got himself a Sprite out of the machine. He stood there drinking it, one hand on his hip. Paco Rojas came around the corner; he threw the key with the wooden board inside the office, landing it on the desk, then came over and pulled a Pepsi out of the machine.

'We'll get some beer down the road,' Chino said.

'I need something else than beer. I can't sleep no more.'

'You looked like you were sleeping.'

'On and off. I should've brought some more downs.'

There was a sound of metal ringing on cement. Paco turned to the entrance of the service area to watch a mechanic changing a tire on a pickup truck. Chino didn't look around. He was staring out at the highway again, south through town, wondering where thirteen hundred and twenty people could be hiding. Slow to 25. And a stoplight at the intersection. They were proud of their stoplights in places like this. Saturday night the people came out and put chairs along the curb and watched the cars stop as the light turned red.

'Five-eighty,' the station attendant said. 'You're all right under the hood.'

'You get the windshield?'

'Yes sir, all the bugs off.'

Chino handed the attendant a bill and followed him into the office. 'You know' – he was going to ask him about the yellow-gut bugs, but he changed his mind and said – 'how far is Trinity?'

The station man looked up from making change. 'That where you going?' When Chino didn't answer but stared at him, the attendant said, 'Twenty-three miles, straight down the road.'

Paco came into the doorway. 'Have him take some Fritos out of that. Some peanuts.'

Beyond Paco, a car was pulling into the station: an old-model Ford sedan that was faded blue purple and rusting out and needed a muffler. Chino watched the people getting out, moving slowly, stretching and looking around. There seemed to be more of them than the car could hold. The station attendant was saying, 'That's not such a good place to go right now. You read about it, uh? The strike trouble?' There were six of them, four men in work clothes and two women, migrants, looking around and trying to seem at ease. One of the women took a kerchief from her head and, raising her face in the sunlight, closing her eyes, shook her hair from side to side, freeing it to the slight breeze that came across the highway stirring sand dust. Two of the men went to the pop machine digging coins out of their pockets. The mechanic came out of the service area wiping his hands on his shirt, squinting as he passed from shade into sunlight. He said in Spanish, 'How much do you want?'

Chino heard one of the men say give them a dollar's worth, please. The woman with the kerchief was approaching the entrance now: a woman who could be twenty-five or forty, a thick body encased in dark slacks, a man's shirt and white earrings set against dark hair and skin. She said, past Paco in the doorway, 'Is there a key you have to the Ladies' room?' Paco turned to look her up and down.

As Paco looked away the attendant, holding Chino's change, began to shake his head. 'No, it's broken. You can't use it. Go down the road some place.'

Both were speaking Spanish. The woman said, 'Maybe it's all right now. Have you looked at it? Sometimes they become all right without fixing.'

The attendant continued to shake his head. 'I'm telling you it's broken. Take my word for it and go some place else, all right?'

'What about the other one?' the woman said. 'The Men's room. She and I can use it and then the men.'

'That one too,' the attendant began.

'Listen,' the woman said, 'we go in separately, you understand? The women then the men. So you don't have to call the police and say we're doing it in there.'

'I can call the police right now.' The attendant's voice was louder, irritated. 'I'm telling you both toilets are broken. You got to go some place else.'

'Where do *you* go?' the woman said. She waited a moment before glancing over her shoulder, feeling the strength of the others behind her. 'No, he doesn't go, this man. Never. That's why he's full of shit.'

The migrants grinned and some of them laughed out loud. The mechanic, standing near them holding a dollar bill, did not smile. He walked into the service area. When he appeared a moment later in the side doorway of the office that opened on the service area, he was holding a tire iron.

Chino said to the attendant who was holding his change, 'When did the toilet break, since we got here?'

'Listen,' the attendant lowered his voice and spoke in English now. 'I got to do what I'm told. Like anybody. The boss say don't let no migrants in the toilet. He say I don't care they dancing around they can taste it, don't let them in the toilet. They go in there mess up the place, piss all over, take a bath in the sink, use all the towels, steal the toilet paper, man, it's like a bunch of pigs were in there. Place is filthy – I got to clean up after.'

'Let them use it,' Chino said.

'I tell you what my boss said. Man, I can't do nothing about it.'

'What are they supposed to do?'

'Go out in the bushes, I don't know. Mister, you have an idea how many migrants stop here?'

'I know what they can do,' Chino said. He looked from the attendant to the woman with the white earrings who was watching him, waiting. 'Hey, he says for all of you to come in here.' When the woman didn't move, Chino said, 'Come in here, will you please?'

As she stood in the doorway, afraid or not understanding, Paco Rojas took her arm and brought her inside, moving her past Chino and the attendant to make room for the others. Paco looked at the mechanic standing in the side door to the service area. He continued to stare at the mechanic as he released the doorstop with his foot and let the glass-paneled door swing closed in the man's face. The mechanic put his hand out, but he stepped back at the last moment to stand removed from them, holding the tire iron, watching dumbly through the glass.

Chino was looking out the main door. 'Come on, all of you,' he said in Spanish. 'The man wants you to come in here, out of the sun. Come on.' He waved his hand to hurry them.

But when they came they filed in hesitantly, bunching inside the doorway, not coming too far, looking at Chino and then at the attendant and then at the woman who was one of them and perhaps understood what was going on.

'Listen,' the attendant said to Chino, 'when you work for somebody you got to do what you're told, right? Man, I like it working here. I don't want to go out and pick onions and cabbage. This is good work.'

Chino was looking at the migrants, at the solemn Hispano-Indian faces and straw cowboy hats and sun-weathered shirts. 'Where are you from?'

One of them said, finally, 'Near San Antonio. We come here for the melons.'

'How much you work for?'

The man seemed surprised. 'I don't know. Whatever they pay.'

'You hear about the strike?'

'Something but not much. We hear people are still working.' The man frowned now, concerned. 'Isn't it true?'

'Maybe this one can tell you,' Chino said, looking at the attendant. 'He wants you to come in and be comfortable.'

'I want them out of here!' The attendant slammed the cash register closed. 'Right now.'

'He says he's sorry about the toilet breaking down,' Chino said.

'They always broken,' the woman with the white earrings said. 'Every place they keep the broken toilet locked so nobody steal it.'

'Listen, I don't say they can't use them,' the attendant said. 'You think I own this place. I *work* here.'

'He says he works here,' Chino said.

The woman nodded. 'We believe it.'

'And he says since the toilets aren't functioning you can use something else.' Chino's gaze moved over the office.

'What are you doing?' The attendant reached out toward Chino's arm, then, realizing it, dropped his hand quickly. 'Listen, they can't use something else. They got to get out.'

'He says use the wastebasket if you want.'

'God Almighty, you're crazy! I'm going to call my boss. Or you want me to call the police?'

'Try and hold onto yourself,' Chino said. 'All right? You don't own this place. You don't have to pay for broken windows or nothing. What do you give a shit?'

The phone was on the desk in front of him, but the Texaco

gas station man with *Gil* over his pocket, who had never been farther away from this place than San Antonio, hesitated now, afraid to reach for the phone or look at it. What would happen if he did? Christ, what was going on here? California Chicano hotshot dude comes in and tells people they can use his *waste*basket. Guy he never saw before. Cold, quiet guy. And the other one –

Chino's gaze moved from the attendant to the migrants. 'He says use the wastebasket. It will be his pleasure.'

They were grinning now, the huddled group, beginning to move and shift their stance and glance at each other, confident of this man for no reason they knew of but feeling it, enjoying it, stained and golden smiles softening their faces and bringing life to their eyes, expressions that separated them as individuals able to think and feel, each one a person now, each one beginning to laugh now at the gas station man and his wastebasket and his boss and his goddamn locked toilets he could keep locked or shove up his ass for all they cared. God, it was going to be something to tell about.

But something else to do. To accept the man's gesture of invitation – arm extended, open hand pointing to the wastebasket – and walk over there and use it, a dark green metal container that would hold everybody's hell, it would hold a gallon from everybody. But to actually use it –

Chino frowned, playing to the group. 'You don't know how, is that it?' He waited. As their smiles began to appear again he walked over to the basket. 'I can show most of you.' He paused then and kicked the metal basket lightly. 'See. Very good construction. Guaranteed.' He glanced over at the group again. 'But a couple of you I don't think I can teach.'

The women giggled, grinning, and the men followed, an audience hanging on to each line and gesture.

Their laughter stopped abruptly as Chino turned his back to them. They waited. The migrants, the station attendant, Paco

Picket Line

Rojas, the mechanic watching through the glass, none of them moved. In the silence that lengthened they could hear a fly buzzing and stunting against the sunlit window. No one looked at the fly.

Paco Rojas said, 'Man, you going to do it or not?'

'Shhhh!' The sound, a woman's voice, came from the group of migrants.

The silence began to settle again, but it was momentary, a few seconds, broken abruptly by the deep drilling sound of Chino's stream striking metal, as if a signal, and at once the migrants were yelling, cheering, laughing, warm and happy and satisfied, relieved, the women giggling, their eyes shining, still hearing the drone coming from the wastebasket. The gas station attendant, Gil, picked up the key attached to the wooden board and handed it to the smiling woman with the white earrings.

3.

Before they had each finished a can of Jax the flat view of sand and scrub had given way to sweeps of green on both sides of the highway, citrus and vegetable farms, irrigation canals and, in the distance, rows of slender towering palm trees that bordered the fields and marked the back roads. In the bottomland of the river valley it was hot early summer: midafternoon now, bright and still and soundless outside the air-conditioned Mercury sedan.

'See,' Paco said, 'right there on the counter they had all these cans of oil and stuff, on the shelves, you know? So if the guy'd started to come in, I mean if he'd touched the door, I'd taken one of the cans and put it through the glass, right in the son of a bitch's face.' Paco grinned. He was in the front seat now, reaching down between his knees to pop the tab off a can of beer.

'You want another one?'

'We're almost there.' Chino's gaze was fixed on the road.

'So, you want a beer or not?'

'I want to eat and go to bed.'

'When're we going to see this guy?'

'I don't know. We look around first.'

Paco took a swallow of beer. 'I got to get me some downers today or I never sleep. Man, if I have to go to Mexico.' He held the can to his mouth again until it was drained, rolled his window down and threw the can out as far as he could.

Then there were billboards in the fields advertising political candidates and car dealers. Then signs for motels and banks. Highway cafes and gas stations and drive-ins, taco-burger stands, a field of junked cars and hubcaps gleaming on the board front of a garage. A stucco motor court from out of the past stood in a grove of palm trees. Signs in front of old buildings announced used clothes, *Ropa Usada*. Railroad tracks crossed the highway and turned south to run parallel with the road, beyond a bank of weeds. A silver water tower against the sky said TRINITY – HOME OF THE BRONCOS. And now, on the right, warehouses and loading sheds lined the train tracks, platformed old buildings that bore the names of farms and produce companies.

'We got a cop on us,' Chino said.

Paco twisted around, hunching behind his arm on the backrest. He studied the white car coming up on them. 'How you know it's a cop?'

'He's been there a while. Now he's making his move.'

'I don't see any light on top.'

'It's a cop,' Chino said.

His gaze dropped from the mirror to the road ahead. There was no traffic coming this way. Chino flicked down the direction signal and swung left off the highway, taking his time, letting the car roll to a stop in front of a chicken and ribs carry-out place.

'How about roast chicken? Buck and a half?'

'He's pulling in,' Paco said.

Chino heard the car approach on his side and skid to a stop in the gravel. He could feel the white car about ten feet away but kept his eyes straight ahead, reading the signs that covered the carry-out place.

Paco was facing him, hunched down to look through the side window. 'Guy must've called them.'

'Take it easy. You want chicken or ribs?'

'Checking the license number now, see if it's stolen. You ain't going to find it there, buddy.'

Chino looked over at the black and gold shield on the car door and the inscription BRAVO COUNTY DEPT. OF PUBLIC SAFETY, then at the man inside who was wearing a neat and official-looking cowboy hat, in profile, studying a clipboard that rested on the steering wheel.

'Sits there in his hat,' Chino said. 'Takes all the time he wants.'

Squinting, Paco's eyes were almost hidden beneath his heavy, scarred lids. 'Maybe he don't want us. No – he's getting out.'

The Bravo County trooper came around the back of his car toward them: beige Stetson and sunglasses, tan pants and shirt, a revolver holstered in a bullet belt and cowboy boots: a big man, middle-aged, slow-moving, solemnly looking over their car. As he reached the window Chino was reading the signs again.

'You get french fries and cold slaw with the chicken.'

'Let me see your operator's license.'

'Or they got barbeque, you don't want chicken or ribs.'

'I think chicken,' Paco said.

Chino nodded. 'That's what I want.'

The trooper's solemn, deadpan expression did not change.

'If you have a driver's license I want to see it, If you haven't, I want you to step out of the car.'

Chino looked up at him. 'What for?'

'All right, get out.'

'I don't know who you are. If you're a cop or a cowboy or what.'

He stared at Chino a moment before stepping aside and motioning to his car. 'You can't read, Pancho, that says Bravo County Department of Public Safety. You spell it backwards it says Police. I can ticket you or I can arrest you, and if you give me any more mouth I'm going to throw your ass in jail. Now do you want to step out of the car or do you want me to pull you out?'

Chino looked at Paco. 'Man wants us to get out.'

'What did we do?'

'I don't know. He don't say.'

'Maybe he tell us if we get out.' Under his breath Paco said, 'The son of a bitch. The hick cop fuzz son of a bitch.'

'Both of you out this side,' the trooper said. He took Chino's driver's license and registration, looked at Paco and said he wanted some identification from him too, then motioned them over to the white car and made them lean against it with outstretched hands while he felt the legs of their pants.

'Listen, you got the wrong ones,' Paco said. 'We don't do nothing. What do people think, drive along, see us like this?'

Chino kept his mouth shut and let the guy search him.

There was a shriek of rubber on pavement close behind them on the highway. A white Olds 98 dipped its hood with the braking sound, hit the gravel and slid to a dust-hanging stop only a few feet behind the Mercury. The Olds bore no markings, but the two men who got out wore Bravo tan outfits, creased Stetsons and sidearms, serious and official, on the job: one with trooper sunglasses and his hat straight and low over his eyes; the other an older man, in his late fifties, moving stiffly, hitching his pants up and holding his belly in.

The trooper waiting with Chino and Paco touched the brim of his hat and said, 'Captain.'

'What've you got, Bob?'

'I got a couple of Franciscos here. Francisco Rojas.' The trooper was looking at their identification, reading from it. 'And the other one, the driver, Francisco de la Cruz. Both of them live in Los Angeles.'

The Captain looked over at the Mercury. 'What about the car?'

'He's got the registration, one in the yellow shirt. In his name. But I ain't looked in the car good yet.'

'What's the charge, Bob?'

'Couple miles north of here,' Bob Almont said, 'I was behind these two, pacin them, and seen them throw a beer can out'n the highway.'

Paco straightened, starting to turn from the car. 'You bust us for throwing away a *beer* can?'

Bob Almont grabbed Paco by the shirt collar and shoved him back against the car. 'I tell you to move, Pancho? Nobody said anything to you.'

Over his shoulder, looking at the officer, Chino said, 'I thought I was Pancho.'

Paco said, 'A beer can, man, like we rob a gas station or something.'

Captain Frank McKellan, stiff and square shouldered, Superintendent of the County Department of Public Safety, an appointed official, a member of the department thirty-seven years, Fourth of July parade leader on a Palomino, President of the Bravo County Gun Club, came over to them. He said, 'You seen the litter barrels, didn't you?'

Chino turned his head, but couldn't see the man, directly behind him now. 'Painted silver,' Chino said.

'That's right.' Captain McKellan nodded slowly. 'We go to some expense to put those barrels all along the road. You know what it costs the taxpayers? Quite a bit. You people come along, you don't pay any taxes. You come down here and work but you don't pay any taxes. Maybe if you did you wouldn't throw your cans and beer bottles out on the road and in the fields. I had a man couple months ago doing some irrigatin for me, cut his hand on a broken bottle somebody heaved out in the field stead of puttin in a litter barrel. Man had to get his hand stitched up and cost him a half day's work.'

Jesus Christ, Chino said, inside, to himself, but hearing it clearly.

'See,' Captain McKellan went on, 'the man that got cut was a Latin, like yourselves, not an Anglo. You see my point? You throw your trash on the highway it's a burden to the taxpayers, but you're also hurtin yourselves.'

'We won't do it again,' Chino said. 'We promise.'

'I want to believe you,' Captain McKellan said. 'You look like an intelligent boy, you're clean, must've worked hard to buy that automobile.'

'Yes sir, worked very hard.'

'You come down here to pick?'

'Yes sir, melons.'

'How come you're not workin in California?'

'Well, just for a change. We go back for the grapes end of July.'

'There's some of you people around here don't believe in work,' Captain McKellan said. 'Sit on their ass and expect to get paid for it. You're willin to work you can get all you want right now. Don't pay no attention to the union.' He paused then. 'You hear about the strike?'

'We heard something.'

'Stay away from those people, do your work, you can make yourselves fifty sixty bucks a week.'

Christ, Chino said to himself, and out loud, 'Yes sir, that sounds pretty good.'

'Bob,' the Captain said then, 'you write up the ticket yet? For litterin?'

'Was just about to when you pulled up.'

'Well – they come all the way from California, Bob, to work – let's let 'em off with a warning this time.'

Bob Almont nodded. 'It's all right with me. I mentioned though I hadn't looked in their car good.'

Chino waited, holding himself away from the police car, staring at the ground in front of his feet.

'Well, I don't know,' the Captain said finally. 'They're not suspects. I think we'll let 'em go. They can get a job and a few hours of work in before the day's over. I know Stanzik's hiring, been looking for pickers since the strike started. You know where Stanzik Farms' at?'

'No sir, but I guess we can find it.'

'Tell 'em I sent you. Captain McKellan. You'll get a job.'

'Yes sir,' Chino said. 'We appreciate it very much.'

4.

'We appreciate it,' Paco said. 'Get a few hours work in, make fifty sixty bucks a week. Man, he's something.' Paco drank from the can of beer he was holding, finished it and threw the can out the window.

They were south of town now, past the main intersection, Main Street, Chino driving slowly, studying the buildings and storefronts on the left side of the highway.

'Yes sir, we appreciate it. Fat cowboy son of a bitch . . . Man, what're you looking for?'

'The union hall,' Chino said. 'Look for a sign says V-A-W-A.'

'Vah-wah.'

'Valley Agricultural Workers Association. We must've passed it.'

'See him tomorrow,' Paco said. 'Man, I got to go to Mexico.'

They checked into the Fun-tier Motel that was pink and had a neon green palm tree sign that would light up at night: one room with two beds for nine dollars. As soon as their suitcases were in Chino pulled off his shirt and shoes and stretched out on his bed. Paco took the car keys and registration, saying he'd be back soon. Chino told him to pick up some roast chicken. They'd forgot all about the chicken. They'd forgot they were hungry.

Paco went out. Chino heard the car door slam. He heard it slam a second time and a moment later Paco was in the room again with a sport coat over his arm.

'We forgot something else,' he said. 'How'd I look going through customs, they find this thing?' Beneath the sport coat he raised from his arm, Paco was holding a .38 caliber Colt Special revolver.

'Put it in your suitcase,' Chino said. 'And listen, find out where Stanzik Farms is.'

Paco frowned. 'What for?'

'Just do it, all right?'

'We going to work?'

'Maybe for a few days.'

'Man, I can't stand that out in the sun. You know it.'

'Paco, get the chicken, will you?'

When he was alone, staring at the ceiling, Chino began to sort it out in his mind and see clearly they would have to go to work for a while.

The cops already had a look at him. If they caught him hanging around, not working, they could make up something and stick him with it. They might even call L.A.

Picket Line

He could go directly to the union hall and see Vincent Mora, lay it on him. Maybe Mora would recognize him, maybe he wouldn't.

But sooner or later somebody would recognize him, at least his name. So it would be good to have some time, study the situation, see what the workers thought of Mora. And the way to do that, go out and pick for a few days. The hell with Paco's punchy head.

5.

It was still cool at six a.m., the vines were wet and darkened the pants legs of the pickers as they worked along the rows with their burlap sacks. Somebody said it was insecticide, the wetness, but most of them knew the field had not been sprayed in several days and that the moisture had settled during the night. Their pants and the vines would be hot dusty dry within an hour. The sun, which they would have all day, faced them from the eastern boundary of the fields, above a tangle of willows that lined an arroyo five miles away. The sun seemed that close to them.

From his pickup truck the foreman, Larry Mendoza, watched his crew working the rows: stooped, round shapes dotting the field, some of the men already ten or fifteen yards ahead of the older ones and the women and kids. There were only eight kids this morning younger than fourteen, a couple of them younger than twelve; he'd had to take them to make up his crew. He'd had to take the Anglo, strong-looking young guy who wore a T-shirt with the name of some university on it. He'd had to take the n— also. But at least the n— had picked before, not honeydew melons, but he had picked and knew what he was doing. The Anglo, Bud Davis, with his muscular arms and shoulders and cut-off pants and tennis shoes – like he was at South Padre Island on his vacation – couldn't pick his nose. He stood up all the time stretching and rolling his shoulders to work the ache out of his back.

This week he had also hired a couple of new guys he had never seen before, from California, asking them what they were doing here when they could make more money at home. The one guy said you want us to pick or you want us to go some place else? Tough guy. He had given his name as Chino and wore a white cloth tennis or fishing hat. Christ, the people you got for pickers. The other guy, Paco, screwed off all the time, hanging around the truck drinking water; but he wasn't the kind of guy you could kick in the ass.

'Hey, how you going to pick melons standing up?'

Larry Mendoza got out of the yellow pickup that said STANZIK FARMS on the door. He crossed the ditch to the field, skinny, hunch-shouldered Chicano striding across the rows, moving toward Bud Davis, the Anglo kid from Dayton, Ohio. The university on his gray T-shirt was Xavier. *Xavier Univ. Athletic Dept.* and a small numeral, 22, in a square.

'I was seein' how much I had in the sack.'

'Fill it,' Larry Mendoza said. 'That's how much you put in. Then you stand up.'

'I'm gettin' used to it already.'

The black guy, Clinton Taylor, working the next row and a few yards ahead, was watching them. Larry Mendoza said to him, 'You need something? You want some help or something?'

Clinton Taylor didn't answer; he turned and went back to work.

'This one' – Mendoza lifted the honeydew from Bud Davis's sack – 'it's not ready. Remember I told you, you pick the *ripe* ones. You loosen the other ones in the dirt. You don't turn them so the sun hits the underneath, you just loosen them.'

'That's what I have been doin'.'

'The ones aren't ready, we come back for later on.'

'I thought it was ripe.' Bud stooped to lay the melon among the vine leaves.

Larry Mendoza closed his eyes and opened them and adjusted the funneled brim of his straw hat. 'You going to put it back on the vine, tie it on? You pick it it stays picked. You got to keep it then. You understand?'

'Sure,' Bud Davis said.

Sure. How do you find them? Mendoza asked himself, turning away from the college kid who had been here three days and would last maybe one or two more, till the end of the week. Walking away, back to the road, Mendoza's gaze stopped on a woman several rows over. 'Hey, mother, where are you, in church? Get off your knees or go home, I get somebody else.' Nobody was paying them a dollar ten cents an hour to rest. Larry Mendoza had started in the fields for forty cents an hour. He'd worked for sixty cents, eighty cents. He was making a buck sixty now as foreman, all year, and drove a pickup truck and his family lived in a house with an inside toilet.

'You hear me? I get somebody else!'

Like it was easy.

The contractor had promised him at least fifty more people – from Mexico if he had to go over there to get them – promised to have them here at six o'clock.

Crossing the ditch Larry Mendoza said to himself, Don't look yet. Wait. He heard Mr Stanzik say, What good is it I pay you to be a foreman you can't get any people?

Then, as he reached the pickup truck, he said, All right, now look. You'll see the bus coming, a whole crew inside, all grown men who know how to pick melons, been picking them since they were boys. Fast? You never seen men could pick so fast.

Mendoza looked and his gaze held. After a moment he was sure of it: yes, something was coming, way down the road, still a couple miles away, coming in from the highway raising dust. But he knew it wasn't the bus. Shit no, that would be too easy for him. He had to worry every day and hire kids and have pains in his stomach. He had to take blame and abuse and a lot of shit from everybody, both sides, and still get the melons picked before they rotted in the fields. It wouldn't be the bus. No chance of it. Though he said in his mind, God, make it be the goddamn bus, will you please and not the strikers?

6.

Well, the sack was full now. He couldn't get any more in it. Bud Davis started across the rows with the sack bumping against his can and the back of his knee, making him walk stiff-legged. Ahead of him the colored guy stood up, twisted his sack closed and laid it gently over his shoulder. Bud took his sack and did the same; it was a lot easier walking. He hurried a little to catch up to the colored guy, following him toward the stake truck that was parked in a side lane about forty yards away. There were a few others heading for the truck: Mexicans who carried their sacks by a shoulder rope and walked stooped over, the sacks almost touching the ground. Yesterday the foreman had caught a kid dragging a full sack and had screamed at him about bruising the melons and fired him on the spot.

'How many you get in a load?' Bud asked the black guy, Clinton Taylor.

'I don't count them,' the black guy said.

'I got thirty this time,' Bud said. 'Figure a pound each – take 'em over to the truck and unload, get a drink, take a leak every once in a while. I bet you make fifty trips a day, fifteen hundred pounds of melons – I don't see how some of those women and little kids make it.'

'They don't count,' Clinton Taylor said. 'That's how they make it.'

'How'd you like to do this all your life?' The guy didn't answer and Bud Davis said, 'I don't even know what I'm doin here. Guy at school said it was good work, not much dough, but you're outside in the sun, get a nice tan –'

He told himself, Christ, watch it, will you? And then told himself, No, it was all right, and tried to think of something else to say, staring at the black round shape of the man's hair.

'You know, get away from home for a while, see some of the country. Maybe go down to Mexico. You had a good time down there?'

'It was all right,' Clinton Taylor said.

He talked to the guy because the guy kept to himself most of the time and didn't seem to have any friends. The Mexicans left him alone, almost as if he wasn't there. But it was sure hard to get anything out of him. All he knew was that Clinton Taylor was from Detroit and had been to Mexico and was broke and needed money to get home.

And the guy sure took his time. Bud had to shorten his stride to stay a few paces behind Clinton Taylor's neat round head and narrow body, narrow hips and the high tight can of a colored halfback, moving like one, like almost all the colored halfbacks he'd ever seen. Clinton Taylor didn't wear work clothes; he wore old clothes that had once been good, sport shirt and continental no-belt pants and regular shoes with thin soles.

'I don't know,' Bud Davis said. 'Bunch of us decided to do it. Then the guys started backin' out. Two of us ended up coming down, took three days hitchhikin, and the other guy went home yesterday.'

They reached the lane where the truck was parked. Clinton Taylor stopped and looked at Davis for the first time. 'Why didn't you go with him?'

'I don't know. I'm here. I go home all the jobs that pay anything'd be gone anyway.'

'You payin' for your school?'

'No, my dad put the money aside for it.'

'Then what're you workin' for, you don't have to pay for nothin'?'

'I got to make my own spending money.'

Clinton Taylor paused, still looking at him. 'You got to make your own spendin' money?'

'Whatever I need for at school. You know – go out on a date, maybe to a show, get something to eat. It cost dough.'

'You go out on a date, huh?'

'Weekends, yeah.'

'They much ass up there at that school?'

'Well, you know, certain girls, ones you know'll go all the way.'

'Is that right?'

'Sure, like any place.'

Clinton Taylor grinned unexpectedly. 'Go all the way. I like to see how far that is, that all the way.'

He turned with his sack of melons and went on to the truck.

Bud Davis followed. 'What else you think I meant? It doesn't matter what you call it long as it's the real thing. Right?'

When Clinton Taylor didn't answer Davis tried to think of something else to say, and then decided the hell with it. Who needed to get put down by a dumb jig melon picker? If the guy didn't want to be friendly, fuck him. He could tell this guy he roomed with a colored guy at school – black guy – who talked to him the same way he did to his colored friends and never pulled any of that superior black bullshit. But it would sound like he was playing up to him, like saying some of my best friends are negroes or blacks or whatever the hell they were supposed to be called now, so Bud didn't tell him.

Clinton Taylor was already up in the truck. Davis went up

the board ramp that had cross pieces nailed to it for footholds and carefully dumped his sack of melons on the pile building in the forward part of the truck bed. As some of the melons rolled down he placed them on top of the pile, making sure they'd stay. He turned and stood up in the hot sun glare to see Clinton Taylor still in the truck, looking off toward the road where a line of cars had stopped and people were getting out.

'Come to save our ass,' Clinton Taylor said.

Bud Davis recognized them from the day before, the same ones with the same V.A.W.A. picket signs, about thirty of them coming up the road, stringing out in single file as they approached the ditch that ran the length of the melon field.

'They always somebody want to save you,' Clinton Taylor said.

Davis watched them spacing out, staying on the other side of the ditch, off company property. The pickets were all looking toward the field now.

'I come here to work,' Davis said, 'and the first thing I know there's a strike on.'

'Nobody makin' you join it.'

'I don't even know what it's about. More money's all I heard.'

'Fifty cents an hour raise and some fringe. They tell the man that's what they want or they walk out. He say go ahead and walk. So stead of getting' a buck ten an hour they get nothin'. You dig it?'

Bud Davis wasn't sure if he dug it or not. There were farm workers on strike and workers still in the fields, so there had to be two sides to it. Or more, counting the growers.

7.

Connie Chavez wore a black bandana tied in back, a pair of gold earrings and a Texas straw hat over the bandana. She wore a denim jacket, levis and sandals and binoculars hanging in front of her on a strap. Connie was twenty, with two and a half years of college behind her and years of working in the fields behind that. Maybe she'd go back to the University of Texas and get her degree in Political Science; maybe not. Today, as a member of the Valley Agricultural Workers Association, V.A.W.A. Local 101, she was on the picket line at Stanzik Farms and the strike – entering its second week – was the realest, neatest scene she had ever been part of.

She raised the binoculars and, for another moment, studied the figures scattered through the melon rows: like a herd grazing in the low vines. When she lowered the glasses, Connie Chavez said, 'Let me have it.' The man next to her handed over a bullhorn.

'Véngase! Para respecto, hombres!'

The amplified words broke the stillness and brought the workers up from the vines to gaze this way, toward the road.

'Come over here, join us. Show them we all stand together for our rights.'

The pickets began calling to the workers, a few by name, motioning them to come over, waving picket signs from side to side, some of them waving red bandanas, twirling them in a circle above their heads.

'Donde están su respecto y dignidad, hombres? Véngase!'

The workers remained motionless, the herd turned and held by the unexpected sound. Most of them had not noticed the arrival of the pickets and they took time now to study the line of people and read the pickets' signs they had read before during the past few days. Several of the signs said V.A.W.A. LOCAL 101 ON STRIKE. And others said UNITE FOR RIGHT! and $1.50 OR NOTHING! and simply *HUELGA!* They watched the pickets as long as they could – taking this opportunity to rest and stretch their backs – until Larry Mendoza came across the ditch waving his arms at them.

'Get back to work! Where are you, at the show? You want to watch those comedians? You don't get paid to watch them or listen to them – you hear me!' They heard him all right, coming across the rows among them, threatening them with the violent motion of his arm, as if cracking an invisible whip.

'No tienen miedo del segundo, hombres! Véngase!'

Connie Chavez aimed the bullhorn at Larry Mendoza. 'Hey, Judas! How much they pay you to kiss Stanzik's ass every day?' She made kissing sounds that smacked loud through the bullhorn and kept at him as Mendoza came back across the field toward the road. 'That how you do it, Judas? He sells his own people for a dollar ten cents and kicks you if you drag the bag on the ground. Judas, you love melons, uh? I hear you go to bed with melons.'

The men on the picket line – there were only a few women besides Connie Chavez – were grinning now and laughing at Larry Mendoza, some of them taunting him, calling him Judas and melon lover. The man next to Connie Chavez said, 'Hey, Larry, your melon got a friend? We go out together, drink some beer.' It was good to relax and laugh. Driving in from the highway a little while ago, approaching the fields, no one had said more than a few words. Now they felt better. Connie Chavez was good; she could talk like a man if she wanted and they never knew what she was going to say.

Larry Mendoza stopped at the edge of the field and stared at them from across the ditch. Until a few days ago he had never seen a picket line. He knew these people and yet now they were like strangers and he wasn't sure how to talk to them.

He said to Connie Chavez, 'Do I insult you? Do I ever call you names?'

Connie raised the bullhorn. 'He asks if he ever insults you. You hear that?'

'I'm talking to *you*, not to them! Listen,' the foreman said,

'I don't care if you strike. Do what you want, but don't bother people who want to work.'

Through the bullhorn Connie said, 'He says he doesn't care if you strike.'

'If *you* strike!'

'If *you* strike.' The bullhorn intensified and relayed the words. The people in the field had stopped working and were looking this way again.

'You don't want to be reasonable,' Larry Mendoza said. 'So why talk to you.'

'He refuses to speak to us,' Connie told the field, 'because we are on strike for a just wage and he doesn't want any of us, or you, to make as much as he does.'

'I didn't say that – I don't *care* how much you make.'

'Judas says he doesn't care how much you make. His own words. All he cares about are the melons.'

'Listen, I care about my job.'

'Judas says he cares about his job, selling people for a dollar ten cents.'

Larry Mendoza waited, staring at Connie, trying to keep control of himself. 'I don't call you names,' he said then. 'You want to strike, it's a free country, go ahead. But don't call me names, you whore, because I do my job.'

'He says it's a free country,' the bullhorn told the people in the field. 'Do you believe that? I'll tell you what's free. The government water the man uses to irrigate his fields. The government money he gets not to grow some kind of crop. But I don't see anybody paying you not to pick the crop he doesn't grow. Do you feel free? Raise your hands out there anybody who feels free. Tell me how many good jobs a Chicano can get in town. You want to pick melons or oranges, that's your freedom of choice. Work for a dollar ten cents, or don't work. How you like living in a free country?'

Picket Line

Larry Mendoza walked over to his pickup truck and got in. They watched the pickup drive off, then swerve toward the edge of the ditch, back up and come around in a U-turn. The pickup shaved them close going past, going somewhere in a hurry.

'There he goes,' the bullhorn announced. 'He says for you to sit down and rest while he goes to the toilet. A nice inside one some place. We ask Stanzik for portable toilets so you don't have to go in the field in front of everybody. You know what he told us? That he can't afford them. Man with five bathrooms inside his house. Lucy Ramirez work there and she count them. Think about it, picking his melons.'

8.

'Somebody need to get in her britches,' Clinton Taylor said. 'Take her mind off the bullshit.'

Bud Davis was across the row watching the yellow pickup streaking out of sight. Gone now, but everybody was working again. He said, 'I didn't realize it was a girl at first.'

'That momma's a girl. I seen her one time, little short dress on, nice ass. Man, it's all there.'

'You know her?'

'I've *seen* her. She don't live at the camp. She work at the union hall for Mora.' Clinton Taylor's gaze returned to the road, to the girl in the straw hat and denims. 'Maybe she givin him pleasure beside work – I don't know nothin about the man.'

'I've heard his name and that's about it,' Bud Davis said. 'The guy organized the union?'

'Pay three dollars to join, go out on strike and he pay you five dollars a week to live on.'

'Where's he get it?'

'I don't know. Strike fund.'

'You ever been on strike?'

'Man, they walk out, I walk away. You don't make no money strikin'. Here you keep workin 'account of Mr Stanzik don't recognize the union. They tell him look, man, we a union that represent all the farm workers. He say shit, you talkin' you ain't sayin' nothin'. They say give us what we want or we go out on strike. He say go ahead, but anybody join the union will never work for him again.'

'Yeah, but what if everybody joined?'

'For what? How these Mexicans feed a family carryin' a picket sign? Man, they all got ten kids. Lady has a kid, the old man come home drunk give her another one.'

'I don't know,' Bud Davis said, 'but if you can hold out – he's got to pay what you want or he doesn't get his crop in. It rots and he loses dough. Right?'

'Wrong.' Clinton Taylor shook his head, trying to get through to this dumb college boy from Dayton, Ohio. 'Even if everybody around here walked out – I mean *everybody* – all the man's got to do is go across the border, five miles away, and get all the Mexicans he want to pick his melons. Man, he only has to pay them people seventy eighty cents an hour, they go home live like kings. Green-carders they call them. Only it's blue.'

'What's blue?'

'The card those people carry. Allow them to come into the country and work long as they want.'

'Well,' Bud Davis said, trying to understand it. 'If Mr Stanzik can get all the people he wants for seventy or eighty cents, what's he paying us a buck ten for?'

'Hey, ask *him*, will you?' Clinton Taylor was running out of interest and patience at the same time. 'I don't know what's in the man's head. They pay me to twist melons, man. That's what I'm doin'.'

Davis filled his sack and took the hundred yard walk to the

stake truck, parked farther down the lane now. There were a couple of pickers up in the truck, so he laid the full sack down gently and went around to where the canvas lister bag hung from the side of the truck. Two workers stood in the strip of shade. The one he had noticed before, with the white tennis hat and the little brim turned down all around, was drinking from the beer can they used for a cup. The other one had soaked his handkerchief with water and wrung it out and was tying it around his forehead.

'That looks like a good idea.'

Neither of them said anything, though the guy with the white tennis hat looked over.

'They ought to have more cups, uh?' Bud Davis said to him.

Chino took a drink and lowered the beer can. 'Why don't you complain?'

'I doubt it would do any good.'

A couple of pickers came around the truck to the water bag. As they stopped, Chino handed one of them the beer can.

'I think I was next,' Davis said.

It was quiet for a moment, in the shade on the off side of the truck, away from the rest of the workers and the picket line up on the road.

Chino said, 'You don't drink after Chicanos, uh?'

'I drink when it's my turn.'

He saw Clinton Taylor come around the side of the truck. Chino glanced over and Bud could see what was in his head right away.

Chino said, 'You don't drink after him either.'

'I said I drink when it's my turn.'

Clinton Taylor stood watching them.

'Maybe the black cat don't want to drink after you,' Chino said to Davis.

One time at school, drinking beer, a guy had taken a cigar out of Bud Davis's mouth, a black guy. Bud asked him for the cigar and reached for it; but the guy held it up over his head, threatening to snap it between his fingers, saying he was too young to smoke, saying he was pretending he was a man, the guy's white teeth grinning at him, trying to get him mad. It was Bud's last cigar, so he wapped the guy in the nose, hard, with a jab from the shoulder, and took the cigar before the guy got any blood on it. The guy that had become his roommate.

He had the same feeling right now he'd had then and said to Chino, 'If you want to argue about who drinks first, I don't see any point in it. If you want to fight over it, I'll knock your fuckin head off.'

Chino motioned to the side and said, 'You want to fight him?'

Davis didn't have to look over to know he meant Paco. 'No, I don't,' he said. 'But if he does your fighting for you then I guess I don't have a choice.'

'You got the weight on him,' Chino said.

'But I've never been in a ring as a pro.' Davis looked over at Paco then; what the hell difference did it make? 'And he has. I bet a lot of times.'

'Eight years,' Chino said. 'Fifty-seven fights.'

Bud Davis was not dumb and felt he knew when to keep his mouth shut, but he had to ask it. He said, 'How many did he win?'

Chino did a funny thing. Without changing his expression or his gaze, the grim, deadpan look seemed to relax. He said, 'Shit, I don't care when you drink,' and walked away.

A little later on, stooped in the rows picking, Clinton Taylor looked across the vine at Davis.

'Hey, you'd have fought that Mexican?'

'If I had to.'

'Mean if you had to? You just say no, I don't want to fight the man.'

'I thought about that at first,' Bud Davis said. 'Then I thought yeah, but what if I could beat him?'

9.

There was a man on the picket line by the name of Luis Tamez who was related to Connie Chavez, an uncle of her mother. He had worked as a migrant for more than forty years, in fields from Texas to Michigan and in Montana. This was his first strike and he was enjoying it, watching the workers fighting the melons, knowing he would never do it again unless they paid him what he wanted. He enjoyed watching Connie and would remember himself at her age and wondered where she had learned so much and why they hadn't done this a long time ago, when he was working in the beet fields for twenty-five cents an hour. Being on the picket line gave him a feeling he had never experienced before. He could stand with his hands in his pockets and look the foreman, Larry Mendoza, in the face and not care what Mendoza was thinking. He could look at a cop the same way – as a police car rolled past – though it was not as easy as staring at Larry Mendoza. He was thinking of the police as he saw Connie coming toward him, passing the others, giving each one a few words.

'No police today. They must be scared of us,' Luis Tamez said.

'It's early,' Connie said. 'They're still in bed.'

'You think they'll come?'

'What else they got to do?' She offered him the bullhorn then. 'You want to play with this, Papa? Tell them a few things.'

'I never use one before.'

'Press the button and talk. It's all you do.' Connie touched his arm then, stepping closer. 'In a few minutes tell them Mora's coming.'

Luis Tamez seemed surprised. 'But he's already here.'

'They don't know it. Say he's coming to talk to them. Have the others start with his name. You know, like we did the other day?'

The old man nodded and she left him, walking behind the pickets, back down the road to where their cars were parked. There were a few people here, getting paper cups of Kool-Aid from a cooler on the tailgate of a station wagon; for the strikers, or for the workers, if they would come out of the field for a cold drink.

Connie Chavez took a cup of Kool-Aid with her and moved down the line of cars to an old-model Volkswagen bus that was a faded washed-out blue, and filmed with road dust: Vincent Mora's field office, that he had brought with him from California six months ago. Connie opened the side door to see him sitting at the table that was covered with folders and papers and magazines. He was holding a pen and had paused from writing to light a cigarette. As Connie stepped inside he looked up – the strange ugly-attractive man with the pock-marked face and the gentle gaze.

'It's hot in here,' Connie said. Sitting down at the table she pushed the cup toward him.

He shook his head but said nothing, watching her as she removed the straw hat and bandana and then the binoculars.

'*Soldadera*,' he said finally. 'Born sixty years too late.'

She saw him watching her and took her hand from her hair. 'Too late for what?'

'The revolution.'

'You didn't hear? There's another one going on.'

He smiled then and it showed briefly in his eyes. 'You did a job on the foreman.'

'If they were all as easy as he is.'

'He hasn't got hold of it yet, what's going on.'

'He got mad this time, called me a whore.'

'What do you want to do, sue him?' Vincent Mora drew on his cigarette. He handed Connie a pad of paper and a pencil. 'Give me some names, people working out there.'

'Some of them you can't tell.' She closed her eyes, as if picturing the field. 'The women with the bonnets, you can't see their faces. There's an Anglo who's been here a few days. Young guy.'

'Chicanos. People that live around here.'

'A chicano who wears a white tennis hat. How does that grab you?'

'What's his name?'

'I don't know, I never saw him before.'

'Just give me a few you're sure of.'

She wrote a name and another one on the pad before turning to stare out the window. It was quiet in the bus. Vincent Mora began writing again. He would look up at the girl's profile, at her hair and the glimpse of a gold earring – studying her, or perhaps looking through her, deep in thought – then would lower his head and continue writing.

When the cigarette smoke drifted across the window Connie knew he was looking up and she thought hard to remember the names of people. Eduardo Ortiz. Ambrocio Varrera. Carlos Leija. Emilio . . . Villescas. She shifted her gaze to the pad and began writing the names and, for some reason, thought of the Anglo boy out in the field, seeing his light-colored hair and gray T-shirt in the glare of the sun. But she could also feel the presence of the man sitting across from her in the little bus. Vincent Mora.

She could see his coarse, heavy features and dark hair that, if you looked closely, was dusted with gray. After working for him three months, being with him almost every day, she still didn't know the man. At first she had thought him too trusting and easy going; maybe even a little slow; a nice guy who was not quite with it. Except that he was an experienced labor organizer. He had worked for the Community Service Organization in Los Angeles and the United Farm Workers Organizing

Committee, also in California, and had been involved in the grape strike and the boycott. He had come here in October and in eight months of talking to workers – in the fields, in cafes visiting them in their homes and gradually gaining their confidence – he had organized over five hundred of them into a union, V.A.W.A. Local 101, and had a week ago called a strike against Stanzik Farms, the largest independent melon grower in the Valley.

He never wore a hat or a tie. Usually an open shirt and a zip-up jacket.

He didn't drink, not even a glass of beer or wine. Though he smoked more than two packs of cigarettes a day.

He was a farm labor organizer who had never worked in the fields. She was certain of that.

He had a name that could be Mexican but he would never be taken for one. Maybe his grandfather had been Chicano. If he was, he had married an Anglo. And his father had married one. Vincent Mora could be German or Black Irish for all she knew.

He was about thirty-eight but looked older, Connie Chavez had decided. In her mind she would not permit him to be as old as forty. She had also decided he was attractive. She couldn't say his scarred heavy-boned face was handsome, no. It was attractive. Unusual. Really interesting. A *man's* face.

What else?

He had never touched her. He had never touched her shoulder or her arm or brushed her hand with his. She had never pictured herself in bed with him. She had thought about it, but she couldn't see it clearly. She couldn't see him with his clothes off. She assumed he was not married. Maybe he had been at one time, she didn't know.

What else?

He never raised his voice.

That was it. A rough-looking man who spoke quietly and was

always composed. It frightened her a little – his restraint. And his awareness – there in the slight movement of his eyes, his gaze shifting to someone speaking, listening patiently, waiting, letting the man run out of things to say, his gaze never wavering or looking away. It was his not speaking more than his speaking or his appearance or his background that described him and formed the picture in the girl's mind. She would wonder what he thought and what he knew that he wasn't telling.

With the sound of the bullhorn Mora looked up and Connie watched him as he gazed out the side windows.

'Mora!' The people on the picket line were calling his name and the bullhorn said, over them, 'Viva Mora! You want to hear the truth? Listen to Vincent Mora. He's coming to talk to you.'

'Lady?'

'What?'

'You told them to do that?'

'Just a little I thought would be all right.'

'Just a little.' His expression and the tone of his voice remained mild. 'But I'm not Juarez. I'm not Villa or Zapata. I'm not the leader of a holy war.'

'I thought, just to get them a little excited –'

'I'm not a spokesman for La Causa or La Raza. I'm not a prophet representing a brown Christ or an Indian Virgin Mary. Am I?'

Outside, the pickets were calling now, 'Viva Mora!' repeating his name in a chant.

'We're not selling me. We're selling an idea.'

'But they like to do it. It gives then a name, a word to use.' She was thinking and trying very hard to explain this. 'You understand? Something to excite them, get them up, instead of an idea they have to think about.'

'The word is *huelga*,' Vincent Mora said. 'Strike. And the word and the idea are the same. It's what we're selling today. The special. Not race or integration, but a strike.'

'If your name helps, why not use it?'

'I'll say it again. I'm not Juarez. I'm not Villa –'

Connie nodded. 'I'm not Zapata.'

'*I'm* not,' Mora said. 'I don't know about you. Whether you want a labor union or a revolution.'

Connie picked up the bandana, pressed it to her head and tied it in back. 'I guess I don't either,' she said. 'Or maybe I don't see any difference. It's for Chicanos. And if we win the Chicanos win. So it's racial, whether we want to think of it that way or not.'

'But it's not how we think of it that's important,' Mora said. 'It's how the Stanzik people think. If they believe it's a race issue they'll say we're rioting and call in the troops – make an emergency out of an incident and send us home. But if we keep this a business matter, then we have a chance they'll come to terms.'

'We're still talking about La Causa,' Connie said. 'These people love the land as much as Stanzik does. But he owns it and they have to live like serfs and he's the lord of the manor.

'Lady – I've read it. I even wrote some of it.'

He watched her shrug and sit back against the seat, maybe tired of talking about it: the twenty-year-old-girl soldier, tough good-looking today girl who in another time might have worn a bandoleer across her breast and ridden for Zapata. He said quietly, 'What do you want to do, burn the man's house down?'

'I've thought about it,' she said and might have been serious.

'And what do you get out of that?'

'A nice warm feeling.'

'You get shot,' Mora said. 'Or twenty years.'

'But they'd know we're here, wouldn't they?'

'Connie Chavez died here. You get your high school graduation picture in the paper. For one day. Tell me, really, why are you in this? For what?'

'I want to help the people. Tell them how it is.'

'Tell them they're poor?'

'*Help* them.'

'Tell them they don't eat the right food and live in filthy shacks and their babies die of pneumonia and malnutrition? They know that.'

'I want to tell them their rights, that they don't have to work like animals for whatever the man wants to pay.'

Mora was nodding as she spoke. He said then, 'You want to win?'

'Of course I want to win.'

'Then tell them what it's like to stand on a picket line.'

She was silent a moment. 'I don't think you can.'

'Tell them what it feels like.'

'I don't think you can explain it. You have to experience being there.'

'Why?'

'Because of the feeling. What it is.'

'So all you have to do is get them to try it. Right?'

Connie was nodding, understanding it now.

'Then it's done,' Mora said. 'Because once a man walks out of the field and joins a picket line, he's never the same again.'

10.

Harold Ritchie had braked almost to a stop and was letting the patrol car roll slowly on its own momentum, bumping along in the road ruts past the line of pickets holding their signs and red bandanas. Every one of them turned from the field to watch him and nobody said a word or moved, though the car passed within a couple of yards of most of them. Beyond the line he accelerated a little, giving the car just enough speed to swing into the side road, and came to a stop in the shade of some bushes close to a cement irrigation tank.

Getting out he took his Stetson from the front seat and put it on carefully, setting the brim an inch above his eyes. On duty a trooper was always supposed to be covered. It made sense; it was part of the uniform; except Ritchie didn't particularly like wearing it. The hat itself was all right – he'd owned a few tan Stetsons in his life – but Captain McKellan made them all wear the hats the same way, the brim curled just a little and pointing straight over their eyes. He'd have curled his more and creased both sides of the crown instead of having just the one groove on top, but it wasn't regulations. After four years in the Marines he'd sworn he was through with regulations. But here he was in a tan uniform again, not as formfitting as a Marine shirt, but with short sleeves which he liked. It showed the tattoo on his left forearm: the snake curled around the dagger and *Death Before Dishonor* in dark blue. The gold-frame trooper sunglasses were regulation.

This was his first close look at the strike. On highway patrol they were told to keep an eye on the union hall and he'd seen the strike signs and the people hanging around outside; but this was the first day he'd been assigned to watch the pickets and keep order. A one-man job it looked like. Nobody would be out to relieve him till after noon. Harold Ritchie took off his hat and reached through the car window to drop it on the seat.

As he walked up the road toward the pickets someone in the line said, 'Hey, come on over here. We need a cop on our side.' Somebody else said, 'Give him a sign to hold!' They watched him approach in that casual cop stride, looking like a cop or a soldier even without his hat: short-haired, good solid five-ten build that showed only a trace of a belly.

Harold Ritchie had lived in Trinity all his life except for the twelve months in Vietnam. Faces in the picket line were familiar. He knew some of them by name. A couple of them he'd even arrested: drunk and disorderly, in a Mexican cafe throwing beer bottles at each other, laughing and swearing and having a hell of a time. He'd gone to school with some of them, or their kids. He'd probably picked crops with some of them too, before he went in the Marines. When he saw Luis Tamez in the line holding a bullhorn he walked over to him.

'What're you doin' here?'

'I'm in the strike. What do you think I'm doing?'

'Papa, you ought to go sit in the shade.'

'I'm in the strike,' Luis Tamez said again.

Someone down the line said, 'Leave him alone, he wants to be here.'

Harold Ritchie looked up, surprised. 'I'm talkin' to the man.'

And someone else said, 'You want to arrest us, try it. We got a lawyer and he say we have a right to be here.'

'I think you're all nuts. I'm talkin' to him,' Ritchie said. 'You understand that?'

'You're police you're for Stanzik,' the man down the line said. 'How much he pay you to watch us? See we don't go on his property. Listen, maybe we don't ever go on his property again. Tell him that for us.'

'That's right,' a woman's voice said. 'We ain't going to work for him again till he pay us what we want and you can't make us.'

What the hell was going on? Ritchie looked at the faces in the line and remembered them as he drove in, the pickets staring silently, not moving. What the hell were they mad at him about?

'You got a gun,' the woman said then. 'Take it out and shoot us, we still don't go in the field. Your gun don't scare us, mister.'

Ritchie said to Luis Tamez, 'For Christ sake, is everybody drunk or something?'

'We're on strike,' Luis Tamez said. 'We got a right to be here if we want.'

'I know you have. What the hell are you mad at me for?'

The old man's expression did not change, or seem to hear or understand. Harold Ritchie had known the man's grandson, the only other person he had met in the Marines from Trinity. They had not been close friends, though they had been close the day he carried the grandson's dead body over his shoulder eight miles out of the DMZ and back to base. After he was home, discharged, he had told the old man about it, some of it, and the old man had touched his shoulder and let his hand rest there while he thought about his grandson and said nothing.

The man down the line said, 'Leave him alone. He don't have to talk to a cop.'

Harold Ritchie walked up close to the man, almost toe to toe, and said, 'Buddy, if you want I'll take that fuckin sign and bust it over your fuckin head and you better fuckin believe it.'

The man didn't say a word, because this cop with his haircut and sunglasses and tattoo on his arm was close and very real.

But someone behind him said, 'Listen how he talks. We got ladies here, he don't care.'

Harold Ritchie had to turn away, his hands tight on his hips, or he might have swung at the man. They were nuts, all of them. Christ, if they really wanted it he could take any four at one time, deck every one of them. But he said to himself, Come on, what's the matter with you? Knowing he had to make himself calm down. It was weird. People he'd known all his life. He saw Connie Chavez over by the line of old cars, then Vincent Mora coming along behind her. Ritchie got to them before they reached the picket line.

'What's the matter with those people?'

Connie's expression was cold, giving him nothing.

Picket Line

'I walk up and they're all over me.'

'You want them to smile and hold their hats? What do you want?'

'They're crazy – I'm talking to old man Tamez, they try and pick a fight.'

'They frighten you, why don't you pull your gun?' Connie Chavez brushed past him, cold eyes and gold earrings beneath a Texas straw hat.

'I don't know,' Ritchie said. 'Maybe everybody's crazy.' He was looking at Mora now, their eyes just about even. From a distance he had judged Mora to be taller and bigger. 'You the one gettin them talkin that way?'

'What way?'

'I thought you were the one for non-violence. I walk up and they try and pick a fight.'

'Why would they want to fight you?'

'Buddy, that's what I like to know. I never in my life had trouble with those people.'

'And they never talked back to you before this,' Mora said. 'Those people.'

'I'm talkin about common ordinary courtesy. I walk up and they start bad-mouthin' me. I come here to keep order, see they don't trespass, and I get all this shit.'

'You want them to apologize?'

'I want to understand it more'n anything else. I *know* those people.'

Mora shook his head. 'No, you don't. Maybe you know their names. But there's no way you could know them, unless you were one of them. Understand that much,' Mora said, 'you'll be doing fine.'

'Buddy' – Harold Ritchie had to turn as Mora started past him – 'I worked with them. Listen, in Vietnam I lived in the same bunker with David Tamez, talked to him all the time –'

But Mora kept going and Ritchie shut up, seeing the people in the picket line watching him.

II.

'Eduardo Ortiz, how're you making it?'

The workers in the field looked over at the sound of the new voice coming from the bullhorn, knowing it was Vincent Mora now.

'Eduardo, we want you to come here and stand with us. Ambrocio Varrera, you also. Carlos Leija . . . Emilio Villescas, all of you come here and show them we stand together. Join the picket line and see what it's like to stand up for your rights.'

Connie Chavez, next to Mora, watched them turn to the rows again and begin picking. Only a few of the men remained standing, looking this way. Through the binoculars her gaze moved over the rows until she found the Anglo, there, coming off the stake truck. He had a handkerchief or something tied around his forehead to keep the sweat out of his eyes. Her gaze moved on and she said to Mora, 'The one in the plaid shirt, over there, that's Ambrocio Varrera.'

'Ambrocio,' Mora said through the bullhorn. 'You think a dollar ten cents is better than nothing? If you do, that's the value you put on your self-respect. A dollar ten cents. Maybe tomorrow they buy it from you for eighty cents. Whatever they want to pay. But if you respect yourself and your family, then join the picket line and tell them what *you* want for a change. See the sign? A dollar sixty or nothing. No pay, no work. No melons get picked.'

'He's thinking about it,' Connie said.

The man in the plaid shirt was standing now.

Mora held the bullhorn on him. 'We'll give you food for your family. We share what we have. We stand together and we're going to win. You want to be with us or not?'

Some of the pickets began to call now, 'Come on, join us!' and wave their signs and red bandanas.

Connie raised her glasses. The Anglo was still by the truck. Doping off. If he was out there to work then why didn't he work? He looked to be about her age. She had gone out with some Anglos at Texas. They had all tried to score the first time and she told them what they could do with it. *Xavier University*. She had heard of the school but didn't know where it was.

The one in the white tennis hat was standing up now, watching – God, that hat was something in a melon field – and a man with him wearing a headband, like the Anglo's, a handkerchief.

She let the glasses slide along the row to Ambrocio Varrera, standing, still undecided.

'The one just behind him, to the right, is Carlos Leija,' Connie said.

The man was hunched down in the vines, but looking this way and watching Ambrocio.

'Ask yourself,' Mora said through the bullhorn, 'you want to be able to say yes, I was on the picket line at Stanzik Farms when we stood together and made them recognize our union? Or, you going to say no, I was out in the field with the kids they had to hire and the scabs and the strikebreakers? You going to tell me you have more respect for a dollar ten cents than you have for yourself? I don't believe it. You're going to tell them to keep their dollar ten, because you're a man and you know it. You know what it feels like.'

'Come on, do it,' Connie said. 'Walk out.' Though only Vincent Mora could hear her.

He said, 'Give him time. The first step's a giant one.' Mora was patient, thinking there was a good chance of getting this one, but not putting all his hopes on it. Each day they had coaxed one or two out of the field, no more than that. They would come out when they were ready; or they wouldn't come at all.

'He's going to do it,' Connie said. 'I know it.' she raised the glasses again to study him and said, 'Move, man, what're you waiting for?'

In that moment, almost as if he heard her, Ambrocio Varrera started across the rows, looking at the pickets and then over toward the police car where the trooper without the hat stood watching him.

'Ambrocio, leave the sack,' Mora told him. 'You don't need it here. Today that's for people who have no respect for themselves.'

The man slipped the rope from his shoulder, letting the sack fall, and came on again.

The pickets cheered, calling his name and waving him toward them, and Mora said, 'That feels good, doesn't it? Like taking off chains.' He could see the man was afraid, coming out of the field alone.

'Carlos Leija,' Mora said then. 'You going to let him walk out by himself? Go with him, man. Keep him company.' He watched Ambrocio look around and now the other man, Carlos, rose and came after him, slipping the sack from his shoulder. All of the other workers were watching now from behind the vines. Only a few were standing. They were thinking about it – they had to be – but none of them moved from their rows as Ambrocio and Carlos walked out of the field.

You have them, Mora was thinking, and felt tired and alone.

Two more who had given up their jobs for him. He could see they were still afraid, but they were committed now and, in having made the decision, already felt some relief and were beginning to smile, each drawing some strength from the other and from the pickets waiting on the road, the pickets cheering and calling their names. They came out of the field directly toward Mora – putting themselves in his hands, their expressions saying all right here we are, we trust you and we did it.

Then it was Mora's turn to smile and extend his hand and give them each a firm grip – showing no trace of the weariness he felt – and say welcome to the Valley Agricultural Workers Association and add their names to the list of five hundred and forty-six members – over three thousand people including their families – who would rely on the union for their daily existance for as long as the strike lasted.

12.

'He's pretty good,' Chino said. 'He grabs them by the balls and keeps pulling.'

Paco said, 'I like the girl. She gave it to that foreman.'

Chino was looking toward the picket line, fifty yards away through the glare, the white brim of his tennis hat turned down all around and low over his sunglasses. 'She don't look like much from here, but she's all right, uh? I like to see her up close.'

'Without any clothes on.'

'Yeah, I bet she don't waste a minute.'

'Let's go find out,' Paco said.

'You had enough of this?'

Paco's expression showed a flicker of hope. 'You mean it? Sure, what good we doing here? Nothing.'

The pickets were bunched around the two men who had walked out of the field. Mora was among them, in the crowd somewhere. Chino couldn't see him now. He said, almost to himself, 'I wonder if he'll know me.'

'What difference does it make?' Paco was anxious now. 'He remember you, he don't remember you, so what?'

'I just wondered,' Chino said. His gaze held on the pickets across the melon rows. He wished there was a side road here that led to the road, so he could walk along taking his time and not have to step over the rows. He should have gone before those two guys. They were up there now and everybody was around them. He should have beat them to it; but he'd been watching the two guys and not thinking about walking to Mora, who didn't know he was here and maybe wouldn't recognize him when he did walk up.

He said to Paco, 'You think he'll know me?'

Paco was about to tell him again, Christ, what difference did it make? But he thought about it a moment and said, 'Sure, he'll know you.'

'It's been six years.'

'It don't matter. He'll know you. Man, he'll be glad to see you.'

'No, we better wait a while,' Chino said, looking at the road again. 'It's not the right time.'

13.

The 98 Olds came up the road doing close to forty. It braked hard and swerved as it reached the line of parked cars, then fishtailed in the ruts and the pickets at the near end of the line jumped back, afraid the car was out of control. It rolled past them and two white patrol cars came in through its dust.

'Stay where you are,' Mora said to the pickets. 'Nothing to worry about. They come to see what a strike looks like.'

The yellow pickup came past them slowly, Larry Mendoza's elbow on the window sill pointing at them while he looked straight ahead. He crept by, giving them time to see the horn-shaped sound speaker in the back of the truck, mounted on a crate against the cab, facing the tailgate.

'Now we get speeches,' Connie said.

'Or entertainment.' Mora watched the truck turn into the side road, where the police cars were parked, back out and turn to face them. 'I think it's hooked to the radio.'

'The idiot, brings the cops to help him find a station.' Connie Chavez raised the bullhorn, turning to the field.

'Attention! *Óigame, señores!* Your foreman has returned from the toilet. Try to look happy while you work for a stinking dollar ten cents an hour.'

14.

The whore, Larry Mendoza was thinking, anxious now to get started. But he had to wait.

Across the ditch standing by the Olds, Captain McKellan was saying, 'What I want to know is where you think you're at.'

'Sir?' Harold Ritchie didn't know what the man was talking about. They were out in a goddamn melon field.

'You're on duty, are you not?'

'Yes sir, I got it on the radio and come right out.'

'Well, if you're on duty, would you mind telling me why you're out of uniform?'

Jesus, he'd forgot all about the hat.

'I guess I left it in the car.'

'You guess you left it in the car.'

'Yes sir, I did.'

'Left it in the car,' the Captain said solemnly. His driver and the two other troopers, one of them Bob Almont, stood over by the irrigation tank waiting, acting as if it was none of their business. Larry Mendoza waited at the side of the pickup truck.

'Your hat is as much part of your uniform as your pants. You wouldn't go out without your pants on, would you?'

Ritchie eased out a little grin. 'No sir, I wouldn't.'

But Captain McKellan wasn't being funny and this tattooed ex-Marine hotshot had better bet his ass he wasn't. He said, 'If we didn't want you to wear your hat we wouldn't have give you one, would we?'

'No sir.'

'Didn't you have to wear a hat in the United States Marines?'

'Yes sir, on duty.'

'But you believe you don't have to working for this department?'

Quit, Harold Ritchie was thinking.

'Well, do you?'

And Larry Mendoza, waiting by his wired-for-sound truck was thinking, Why did you call them? Official gringo cop bullshit. Yes sir, no sir. If he had known Harold Ritchie was already out here he wouldn't have called.

'Yes sir.'

'You *do* believe you don't have to wear it?'

'I mean no sir, I don't believe you *don't* have to wear it. I believe you *do*.'

Get in and blow the horn, Larry Mendoza thought. God, that would be good if he could do it. But he'd have to be drunk and quitting the next day.

'Harold, you been with us what, about two years?'

'Twenty-eight months this week.'

'Harold, I been in the Department thirty-seven years. Not once, in that time, have I ever been on duty without my hat on.'

Run, Harold Ritchie thought, but found himself nodding thoughtfully, not sure what he was agreeing to.

'Well, that's all I'm going to say,' Captain McKellan said. 'Harold, you've got a good record. You've served your country.

I just don't want to see you beginning to acquire a bad attitude and fuck up your life. If you know what I mean.'

'No sir, I don't want to do that.'

'Then put on your hat, son, and let's go to work.'

Larry Mendoza hopped inside the pickup, turned the key and revved the engine, ready to go. Captain McKellan came up on the passenger side, where the wires trailed in from the speaker and hooked beneath the radio: the official face of a police superintendent wearing his hat and tinted glasses, framed in the side window.

'You sit tight, you understand?'

'Why don't I go by them once? Show them what I got?'

'Because I said to stay here.'

Tell him who you work for, Mendoza thought, but couldn't say it. He nodded and watched Captain McKellan start down the road toward the picket line, taking his time, followed by his four troopers with their hats on straight over their eyes.

15.

Bob Almont told Mora and the pickets what they had to do. First, move over to the other side of the road, away from the field being worked. And second, space out so there would be ten feet between each person. Vincent Mora said there was no statute that required pickets to do this. Bob Almont said he didn't need a statute, he was telling them. And if they didn't obey this minute they'd be arrested and charged with unlawful assembly. Harold Ritchie and the other two troopers stood facing the picket line with Bob Almont. Captain McKellan stood off by himself; he didn't see the need to speak to these people directly.

He watched as his troopers moved the pickets to the other

side of the road and spaced them out, extending the line almost up to the police cars on the side road. When he saw Mora coming over, walking right up to him, he couldn't believe it.

'What's this for?' Mora asked him.

McKellan was looking past Mora, along the picket line. 'I believe the trooper explained it.'

'Can't I ask you?'

'You congregate out here like a mob, we'll arrest you for unlawful assembly, enciting to riot, causing a disturbance or anything I feel we can make stick. Does that answer your question?'

'No, I asked you what's this for. Why are you doing it?'

'I just told you.'

'We haven't broken a law.'

'And we're here to see you don't.'

'Look, we haven't done anything –'

The Captain was facing him now, staring, and Mora knew he wouldn't be able to talk to him. The Captain didn't understand, because he did believe he had answered the question. It would take years to get through to him, to make him see his own point of view; or else it was already too late. Mora said, 'You have any Chicanos on your force?'

'Latins? We have a number of them. Why?'

'Why don't you send some of them out here?'

'I've never talked to you before this,' Captain McKellan said. 'I hope I don't have to again. I hope you get done whatever it is you're doin here and go back to where you come from.'

'Can I ask you one more question?' Mora waited, making the man say something.

'What is it?'

'Do you think I'm a Communist?'

The man stared at him, the lines in his face hardened as he restrained himself to remain civil and not lose his temper.

'Well?' Mora said.

And the Captain answered, 'You said it, mister, I didn't.'
Mora smiled. He turned and walked back to the picket line.

16.

Connie Chavez picked out a woman in the field and pressed the trigger of the bullhorn.

'That's your little boy carrying a sack of melons bigger than he is? You don't care, uh, if it deforms him for life? Stanzik doesn't care either. Why should he care about your children if you don't? Hey, what's he pay them, fifty cents? That's how much more he should pay you. Then your children don't have to work. Think about it while your child is getting bent out of shape. *Señora, tiene que –*'

The sudden blast of music drowned out the rest of her words and she saw the people in the field, all of them, look up. She turned then to see Vincent Mora in the road, stepping out of the way, and Mendoza's yellow truck coming toward her, rolling slowly past the picket line, bringing the high-volume, intensified sound of a girl singing, with full orchestration, 'Who Can I Turn To?'

She saw Larry Mendoza smile at her as he went by and saw the speaker, in the back of the truck, that was blaring the song at them. The truck continued on, past the parked cars, to an open area of road where Mendoza stopped to turn around.

Connie raised the bullhorn.

'Now they give you music,' she said to the people in the field. 'You get music instead of a fair wage. It's very nice, but you can't eat it, can you? Try to feed your family with music. Try to buy bread –'

The truck returned and the girl's voice, winding up the song, telling them she had no one to turn to, covered Connie's words. Connie waited. She liked the song and she thought maybe the girl singing it was Vikki Carr. When the truck was beyond the picket line, approaching the side road where the five men in uniform stood by their white patrol cars, the volume dropped and there was the faint sound of the disc jockey's voice or someone delivering a commercial. Connie aimed the bullhorn in that direction.

'Hey Judas, you square, get XECR, Reynosa! We want to hear some rock!'

To the people in the field she said, 'If you have any requests give them to the gentlemen over there in the uniforms. They work for Judas. Tell them what you want to hear.'

The radio volume increased abruptly and Mendoza's truck came at them again, bringing to the picket line and the melon fields the ornate piano styling of Roger Williams and 'Falling Leaves'.

17

Just before noon, Captain McKellan and one of the patrol cars drove away, leaving Harold Ritchie and Bob Almont to watch the pickets and keep them spaced ten feet apart. Bob Almont made up another rule. He said if they wanted a drink of water they had to get it one at a time. If there was any milling around that station wagon he'd have to arrest them for unlawful assembly. Mora didn't say a word. He got a cardboard box full of sandwiches from the wagon and passed them out to the pickets. Then he got the cooler and carried it up and down the line pouring a cup of Kool-Aid for whoever wanted one. Bob Almont watched him and said to Harold Ritchie, 'I'm goin tangle with that one before we're through. You wait and see.'

Ritchie said, 'I don't know what they want to stand out in the hot sun for. It ain't doin' them any good.'

After a while he got tired of all the oldies but goodies Mendoza's radio was playing and when the truck stopped to turn around, Ritchie said to the foreman, 'That wasn't a bad idea Connie had. Why don't you get XECR for a change?'

Mendoza said maybe later; he had to go back to the yard and call the labor contractor. After he left it was a relief to have quiet again. But it wasn't a minute before Connie Chavez had the bullhorn going, talking to the workers who were sitting around by the stake truck now, eating their lunch. Ritchie didn't listen to her at first. He was hungry and thinking about where he'd go eat when the relief man got back. Then he caught a word and began listening to her.

'How does it feel, Anglo, to take a poor man's job? Take food out of the mouths of his children. You get enough to eat. That's all you care about.'

18.

'She talkin' to you,' Clinton Taylor said.

'I didn't take anybody's job.'

They were sitting on the tailgate of the stake truck eating their lunch. Bud Davis had a couple of fifteen-cent grocery store pies, a peach and a pineapple, and three packs of peanut butter cheese crackers. He was frowning, squinting in the sun glare, to hold his gaze on the girl in the picket line. From here he couldn't even tell she was a girl, except that he knew her voice now. After a moment he turned on his side and eased back to support himself on one elbow. The peach pie was good; he should have brought about five more.

'We see you,' the bullhorn said.

Abruptly he pushed himself up to look through the spaced side boards of the truck body.

'You can hide from us,' the bullhorn continued. 'But you can't hide from yourself. You know what you've done.'

'What the hell she talkin' about? I'm not trying to hide.'

'She's picked you out to work on.' Clinton Taylor looked over at the road, his tablespoon poised in the air. He was eating cold Franco-American spaghetti and meatballs out of a can.

'She must mean somebody else.'

'She ain't talkin' to me. And everybody else I see is Mexican.'

They were scattered about in small groups, most of them on the off side of the truck where the waterbag hung, sitting in the narrow strip of shade, eating sandwiches and packaged baked goods and beans and chili from cans. They brought their lunches with them, all but a few whose children came out at noon with containers of hot food and tortillas and TV dinners. And usually they drank cold pop that Larry Mendoza's brother brought out in his car and sold to them for twenty-five cents a can.

'Hey, Anglo, what do you do with your money? Spend it on beer and girls?'

Some of the workers sitting on the ground near the truck looked up at Bud Davis, as if expecting him to answer. The guy in the white hat and his buddy, the fighter, were drinking beer and watching – sitting in the sun drinking a six-pack.

'What she pick me out for?'

'She tellin' you,' Clinton Taylor said. 'Listen to her.'

'She doesn't even know me.'

'The man whose job you took,' the bullhorn voice said. 'You know what he'd spend it on? Food for his family. Clothes for his little children. Used clothes, because that's all he can afford. *Ropa usada*, Anglo. You see the stores on the highway where we have to buy somebody else's old clothes because the man won't pay us enough. You wear used clothes, Anglo, at that Xavier University?'

'How'd she know that?' Christ, he felt like he was on a stage.

'What do you need a job for?' the bullhorn asked. 'Your daddy pay for your school, doesn't he?'

'She don't know you,' Clinton said, 'but she sure reachin you.'

'Likes to hear herself talk,' Bud Davis said.

'Anglo, stand up so everybody can take a look at you.'

He didn't move. He felt the workers near the truck watching and took a bite of peach pie. Several more workers came around from the off side to see what he was doing.

'Come on,' the bullhorn coaxed him. 'They can't see you hiding in the truck.'

That was enough. Bud reached above him, grabbed a side board and pulled himself up.

'There he is!' the bullhorn announced, and some of the pickets cheered and waved their signs. Bud watched them, he finished the last bite of pie and waved back, raising one arm straight up in the air.

19

From the road Connie could make out a raised arm, but she had to bring up the binoculars to see the detail of his gesture, his hand in a fist and the middle finger pointing to the sky. She said, Screw you, too, buddy. But she also smiled, lowering the glasses, and felt a little rise of expectation, of almost excitement.

He disappeared behind the bullhorn as she said into it, 'Hey, Anglo, what do you want to pick melons for? Big strong boy like you – you should be holding a sign. Come on over here. See if you can lift the one that say *Huelga*. You take Spanish at that school? It means *strike*, Anglo.'

She studied him again through the glasses. His arm was down and he was eating something, still looking this way, leaning on the side rail the way you would stand at a bar or a counter. Relaxed and sure of himself. Or else pretending it. Connie wasn't sure; but she had a feeling she could bring him out of the field if she nudged him with the right words, needled him gently and worked on his pride. Once they were standing up it was hard to let them go.

Through the bullhorn she said, 'They teach you anything about trade unions in college? How about the National Labor Relations Act? It says workers have the right to organize a union, present grievances and strike if necessary. But not farm workers. All other workers can have a union except farm workers. How does that grab you?'

He was still on the truck, listening, still looking this way.

'Think about it. Why are farm workers different than other workers? Why can't we go to federal court and make Stanzik recognize our union? Why can't we make him sit down with us and listen –'

And she was cut off – with the Anglo still out there hanging on her words – by the intensified twangy sound of a Country and Western melody. The yellow pickup had rolled in without her hearing it and was almost in front of her when the music blared out of the speaker and filled the air with Merle Haggard's 'Okie from Muskogee'.

20.

A Stanzik foreman by the name of Ray Doyle was driving the pickup. As soon as he spotted Vincent Mora in the line he came to a stop, got out and walked away from the ear-shattering sound. He saw Mora raise a hand to get his attention, but Ray Doyle ignored it and made the man come after him.

Mora said, almost shouting, 'You want to turn that down a little?'

Picket Line

Doyle gave him a look, only that. And when Mora stopped, Doyle kept walking, looking at the faces in the picket line now, telling them with his gaze, I know who you are and I'm going to remember it – giving each one a cold squinty stare, not saying a word to any of them, though he knew them all by name. Doyle wore a Texas straw hat and a striped T-shirt to show off his stocky build, his thick short arms hanging away from his body, and barely moving as he walked over to the police cars.

Ritchie said to him, 'What happened to Mendoza?'

'That dumb bastard,' Doyle said.

He nodded to Bob Almont who was sitting on the front fender of his patrol car. He didn't know Almont too well, Almont was older. But he had gone to high school with Harold Ritchie and played football with him, though they hadn't hung around together too much.

'He was suppose to have fifty more people out here this morning. I sent him down the bridge to look for the goddamn labor contractor.'

Abruptly, in the middle of a mournful note, Merle Haggard stopped singing. The two troopers and Doyle, all three of them at the same time, looked over to see Mora standing by the pickup.

'If he fooled with your truck,' Bob Almont said, 'you can make a complaint.'

Doyle was already walking away from them. Harold Ritchie said after him, 'Ray, if you turn it back on, get XECR, all right?'

Ray Doyle didn't give the pickets his look going back past them. He kept his eyes on Mora who was standing in the road waiting for him.

'You keep your hands off Stanzik property,' Doyle told him as he approached.

'I did it for you,' Mora said. 'To save the battery. I thought you maybe forgot you left it on.'

Ray Doyle didn't see anything funny. He said, 'You stay away from this truck.' Then looked over at the two troopers. 'They're supposed to stay over the side of the road, ain't they?'

Bob Almont nodded and called back, 'Else they'd be obstructing traffic.'

Doyle said to Mora, 'You hear him? You stay over there and you don't move. Understand?'

'How about this?' Mora said. 'You don't play the radio for a while, we won't play the bullhorn. Everybody take a rest.'

As Doyle brushed past him and got in the pickup Mora knew there was no way to talk to the man. He was stubborn or had no sense of humor or was simply stupid. Like Captain McKellan. Like, God, so many of them. The truck started up and he had to get out of the way. As it shot past him the sound of a Nashville girl, with a hopeless sob in her voice, pierced the stillness. There was static then and quick pieces of sound as the selector ran through several stations, came to a wailing blues rock male voice and stayed there.

21.

Leon Russell, Bud Davis said to himself. He was pretty sure, though he couldn't think of the name of the piece he was doing.

'How'd you like to be up on the road hearing that?' he said to Clinton Taylor. They were in the rows again working, twisting the ripe melons from the vines, down in the dirt again, in the heat and sweat of a summer harvest.

'I can hear it fine from here,' Clinton Taylor said. He looked up, resting on his heels for a moment. 'The sweet sound of Doctor John the Night Tripper.'

'Uh-unh, it's Leon Russell.'

'What you talkin' about, Leon Russell?'

'I think it is.'

'It's Doctor John, man, don't you know that sound?'

Bud Davis was kneeling up now, watching. He said it again, though only to himself this time, How'd you like to be up on the road? That's where it was going on. It was like the people in the field were here to watch the activity on the road. He'd like to sit in the shade and watch it a while.

He'd like to get a closer look at that girl with the bullhorn. He wouldn't mind talking to her either.

He said to Clinton Taylor, 'I'll bet you five bucks it's Leon Russell and not Doctor John or anybody else.'

22.

Ray Doyle took the truck up the road past the troopers' cars, turned around and came back with his foot mashed down on the gas pedal, aiming the truck directly at the pickets and then cutting it just enough to skim past them and see the awful look on their faces as they saw him and pushed and threw themselves out of the way. He gave them a safety margin of about a yard on the first pass.

He drove about a hundred yards down the road toward the highway, letting them begin to think he was leaving, before turning around and coming back at them again, cutting it a little closer this time, catching a glimpse of Mora with his arms outstretched as if to hold the people in line; but their eyes were on the truck, not Mora, looking defensively over their shoulders at the front fender and headlight coming at them and most of them moved well out of the way to make sure the truck wouldn't hit them. They grimaced and waved at the dust that rose in the truck's wake, dust and flying gravel and the heavy sound of the rock music on top of them and then past them and now Mora looking up and down the line, telling them to hold their ground.

'Stay where you are!' he called in both directions. 'He's not going to hit anyone, he's trying to scare us. Stay where you are and try not to move.'

He was aware of the cops standing by the patrol cars with their arms folded, keeping out of it. That was all right. Maybe they could show the cops something in the way of guts – 'Look, we're serious.' – that would impress them and open their minds a little. He was also aware of the people in the field watching and they were more important. He knew he could win some of them if the picket line would hold and not come apart. But it was their first test in the presence of physical danger and he wasn't sure of them. So he knew he would have to show them himself – by taking a half step into the road and standing with his hands on his hips, seeing the truck coming again and hearing the scream and wail of the music increasing, seeing the truck coming right at him, then making himself look out at the field the moment before the rushing sound and the dust and the outside rearview mirror grazed past within inches of his face. It was easier to stand and not move when the truck came back, because there was no rearview mirror on the right side.

On the next pass some of the pickets held their signs out in the road and waved them, as if to taunt or provoke the truck, giving it something to aim at, then jerking the signs out of the way as the truck rushed past.

'Don't fool with him,' Mora called to them. 'When an idiot gets angry you don't know what he might do.' They grinned and nodded; they were getting used to this and were more relaxed. Mora said, 'Stand where you are. That's all we have to do.'

As the truck came at them again, Mora's body tightened. He didn't realize he had closed his eyes until he opened them as the truck passed and he saw the truck skimming close to the pickets and saw a man in a plaid shirt near the end of the line holding a red bandana in his two hands, in the formal pose of a matador offering the bull his cape – Ambrocio Varrera, one of the men who had come out of the field. Mora recognized the man the moment before the right fender of the truck caught the man's right side – as he tried to push away from the impact – and slammed him thirty feet down the road and into the ditch. The truck had swerved at the man, Mora was sure of it.

The sound of the speaker went off abruptly. The truck was still moving up the road, but slowly now, as if Ray Doyle, the foreman, wasn't sure what he should do and was making up his mind or giving the police time to stop him.

Mora got to the man in the ditch as the two troopers came across the road and Bob Almont, pulling a leather book from his hip pocket, said to the people crowding around Ambrocio to get out of the way and let him through. Mora could see Ambrocio then and Connie Chavez, bareheaded already in the ditch, sitting so that she could support the man's head on her thigh. There was blood on the side of his face that Connie was touching gently with her bandana. Ambrocio seemed stunned, his eyes open but glazed. Mora could see that the man's right leg was broken between the knee and the hip.

He said to Bob Almont, 'It's called assault. I don't know what kind of assault, but that's what it is and you saw it.'

Bob Almont had the leather book open and was writing. 'No, what I saw is called obstructing traffic, and soon as somebody tells me what his name is, I'm goin' to give him a ticket for it.'

23.

'I don't know,' Chino said. 'Man gets knocked on his ass they firm the line again, asking for it. Why don't they pull the guy out of the truck?'

One of the pickers, a young man about twenty, said, 'That's Ray Doyle. He's a foreman.'

'So what he's a foreman?' Chino said. 'He hit the guy. You saw it.'

There were a number of pickers near Chino, in the rows behind him and in front of him, all watching now as a station wagon drove off with Ambrocio Varrera in the back end. A few hours earlier he had been in the field with them.

'I think that strike leader went with him,' Chino said. 'Very kind person. Or he's getting out of there so it don't happen to him.'

The young picker who had spoken before said, 'They believe in him. You talk to people, they say he knows what he's doing.'

Chino turned to look at him. 'What're you still working for?'

'I haven't made up my mind yet,' the young guy said. 'But I think the strike's a good thing.'

'You don't want to stand around in the road for nothing,' Chino said. 'That's the way I see it too. If you got a bitch against the foremen or the grower, then do something, don't stand there. Right?'

'That's right,' the young guy said.

'Show them you mean business,' Chino said. 'Maybe come out here at night, stomp a few acres of melons, kick 'em in or smash 'em with clubs.'

'That'd be something,' the young guy said. 'The foreman comes out in the morning, finds all the melons smashed to hell.' He grinned thinking about it.

'There are all kinds of ways,' Chino said.

24.

Luis Tamez had been next to Ambrocio in the line and had seen the man take a stance, hands on hips, facing the direction from which the truck would come, and had told the man to put his feet together and hold the inside edge of the cape against his right hip, and the man had grinned and said yes, that's what it was like, except the truck didn't have horns. Sure it had a horn, Luis Tamez said, but not the kind that could hurt you. The man had grinned at that also and said he wished he had something to cape the truck with. So Luis Tamez had given the man his red bandana that he had been waving all day at the field workers. He had seen the man's expression when the truck hit him and had seen the red bandana go up in the air, but he didn't see it anywhere now.

They made a bed in the back of the station wagon with two car seats and a blanket and drove off with Ambrocio to the hospital. No one had asked the police to help them, to take the man in their car or lead the way with their siren. The hell with the police bastards. They had actually given the man a ticket and had threatened to arrest anyone who continued to object and yell at them in Spanish, saying they were obstructing the law. The other one, not Harold Ritchie, did this; though Harold Ritchie was there and didn't argue with him. And it was strange that Mora didn't argue with the policeman. He said a few words to him, then spent his time with the man, Ambrocio Varrera, and had gone with him in the station wagon to the hospital. They were to form the line again and say nothing to the policemen.

With the bullhorn Connie Chavez told the people in the field what had happened. 'Did you see it? That foreman deliberately ran over Ambrocio Varrera. That's the kind of man you work for? He runs over the father of children and puts him out of work because he joined the union.'

As Connie Chavez continued to talk to them, Luis Tamez watched the foreman Ray Doyle, who was over by the side road with the policemen, talking to them but most of the time looking this way, his hands on his hips. Now saying something to

Harold Ritchie. Harold had always been pleasant and courteous, a friend of his grandson killed in Vietnam; now he was a policeman and he was different. Luis Tamez was thinking, Why are policemen different? What changes them? He saw Ray Doyle coming toward the picket line.

The foreman kept to the field side of the road and stopped about twenty feet away from Connie Chavez, the only one he was looking at, staring at her with his heavy arms hanging ready, hands curled open as if he might come over and grab her. Connie ignored him until he raised an arm and pointed at her.

'You put that away, you hear?'

Through the bullhorn Connie said to him, 'This thing? You don't like it?'

'I'm tellin' you, put it away.'

'Or what,' Connie said, 'you run over me?'

'That man stepped in the road,' Ray Doyle said. 'He was foolin' around and it was his own fault he got hurt.'

'Come on,' Connie said, 'Get your truck, let's see if you can do it again.'

'I'll take that thing away from you is what I'll do.'

'Now your foreman threatens me,' Connie said to the field. 'How do you like to work for someone who assaults women?'

Luis Tamez watched the foreman turn and walk away and knew the man was burning with anger and that it was going to begin again and the man wouldn't be able to control himself. Luis Tamez was certain of this; but what incensed him more was the confident way the man walked, so sure of himself with his tight T-shirt and muscle and cowboy boots, not caring what was behind him or what they thought watching him.

No one saw Luis Tamez go to his car and start it and work it out of the line – a '54 Chevy that had traveled 160,000 miles on three engine blocks and nearly two hundred used tires. They didn't see Luis Tamez until he was driving past the picket line and the foreman had reached his truck that was nosed into the side lane and almost broadside to the road. The foreman had the door open and was getting in when Harold Ritchie yelled out and Doyle looked around to see the '54 Chevy coming at him. He hung there between the open door and the seat as if he might jump out and run for it. But it was too late and he knew it and he was barely able to get inside before the Chevy, doing about thirty, slammed into the door and the side of the truck. With the wonderful sound of the crash a spontaneous cheer broke from the pickets. They waved their signs and yelled as loud as they could as Luis Tamez backed off and rammed the truck again, turning the front end into the ditch. They yelled at him to hit it again, hit the son of a bitch. But Luis Tamez had to swerve to avoid hitting Harold Ritchie who was in the road now and when he slammed into the truck's rear fender this time he hooked his bumper and the troopers dragged him out of the car.

For a moment he couldn't believe it had happened – until he heard the cheering and the people calling his name. Then he was grinning and trying to wave to the pickets as Harold Ritchie and Bob Almont held him and finally got the handcuffs on him. Harold Ritchie said, 'God Almighty, Luis, what's the matter with you?'

'Cop,' Luis Tamez said. 'You want to arrest me, do it. Quit talking.'

He was grinning again – his face showing in the side window – as the patrol car drove out past the picket line.

25.

The union hall was a storefront on the highway with a sign painted on the plate-glass that said V.A.W.A. HEADQUARTERS. Chino decided he must have been watching the cop tailing him and that's why he didn't see it coming into Trinity. He remembered the used clothes store and the run-down stucco tourist court on the north side of the union hall. He had left Paco asleep in the room at the Fun-tier Motel. It was past eight o'clock now and full dark.

The place was lit-up inside and there were more than a dozen people standing around and sitting on the folding chairs along the side walls. Some of them looked at him as he came in. Maybe they had been out there and remembered his white hat. He walked to the counter that divided the hall part of the room from the office area and asked a girl behind the counter for Vincent Mora. She said he was out, but should be back soon. He looked closely at the girl and knew she wasn't the one with the bullhorn.

There were V.A.W.A. strike posters on the walls and the face of the counter, travel posters of Spain and Mexico and hand-lettered announcements – *Tondo El Mundo esta invitado que venga a la Resada* . . . There were newspaper pages with columns marked in red. There was a photograph of Emiliano Zapata on the wall behind the counter and a statue of the Virgin Mary on a stand.

There was one vacant seat. Chino took it and sat there smoking a cigarette and reading the announcements about the twenty-five-cent meals and day care for the children of the strikers and one that said, 'Our kids don't have blue eyes, but they go overseas to fight!' There was a lot of crap like that on the wall to read. He'd seen plenty of it. As soon as there was a reason for an organization somebody would start making posters and soon the walls would be covered with them. A person says sure, I'm fighting for La Causa, and ask him what he does and he says man, make posters, what do you think?

When Connie Chavez came in Chino knew right away who

she was. No hat now. Tight jeans and a T-shirt. Not as good-looking as he thought she'd be, but not bad. About five-three, nice little can that stuck out and real tits. She needed to fix her hair though and put some of that stuff around her eyes. She looked washed out and tired, like she'd been picking melons.

Vincent Mora, behind her, looked older. Not six years, about sixteen years older. Tired-looking and showing some gray in his hair, but the same ugly horse face and the cigarette in his mouth – coming in nodding and trying to look pleasant, touching people on the shoulder. Several of them were talking at once, asking him questions, and he had to hold his hand up for quiet.

'Ambrocio's going to be all right –'

Someone said, 'They let him in the hospital?'

'He's in the hospital,' Mora said. 'Luis Tamez is in the county jail charged with felonious assault, and if anybody's got five thousand dollars on them we can get him out.'

He answered questions about Ambrocio and Luis Tamez and was telling them about seeing Ray Doyle, the foreman, in the emergency ward of the hospital – turning and looking around to talk to all of them – when he saw Chino. Mora paused and his gaze lingered.

Connie Chavez was behind the counter now. She saw it, Mora's expression, and recognized the man in the white hat. Then Mora was telling them Ray Doyle had needed eight stitches over his right eye and had a terrible headache and maybe a sprained wrist. Everyone grinned and cheered. As they began talking to each other Mora turned to the man in the white hat again. A moment passed before the slight smile of recognition touched his face, acknowledging that he knew the man.

'Francisco de la Cruz,' Mora said. 'Chino.'

Now Chino was smiling a little, not giving it too much. 'I wondered if you'd remember.'

'How many did you bring?'

'Guys? Just me and a friend. We heard about the strike you know so we come see what's going on.'

'Working in the field – that's a new one.'

'It wasn't bad, a few days. I got to talk to the people, see what they think.'

Mora waited a moment. 'How'd you like some coffee?'

Chino nodded. 'Yeah, Father, that'd be fine.'

Mora stared at him and there it was again, the tell-nothing expression. Connie saw it. She watched Mora turn and walk away and the one called Francisco de la Cruz, Chino, follow him around the counter and into Mora's office. She had heard the name before. Chino. Something she had read with his name in it. A newspaper clipping in Mora's file. Chino de la Cruz.

She said to the other girl at the counter, 'What did he call Vincent? Did you hear him?'

The girl shook her head. 'No, I didn't. Why?'

'I thought for a minute,' Connie said, 'he called him Father.'

26.

'It slipped out,' Chino said. 'From habit.'

'Chino, nothing has ever slipped out of you in your life.'

'They don't know, do they? You haven't told anybody.'

'What difference would it make?'

'Maybe it would scare them a little. They respect you more.'

'I'm no longer a priest,' Mora said, sitting across the second-hand desk from Chino in the ten-by-ten-foot office that was windowless and had only a calendar and a crucifix on the walls. 'I haven't worn a collar in eight years, so why bring it up? I could have been a streetcar conductor or worked in a factory.'

He stopped as Connie Chavez came in with two cups of coffee

and placed them on the desk. She looked at Mora. He thanked her, and when he said nothing else she left and closed the door.

'You keep it a secret from her too?'

Mora lit a cigarette. 'There's a difference between not telling something and keeping it a secret. If people find out, all right, what difference does it make? I was ordained five years and that's all, no mystery. It's done all the time these days.'

'You're worried about something.' Chino picked up his coffee and blew on it. 'Or, you're wondering what I'm doing here.'

'I'll admit it crossed my mind.'

'I'm going to help you. I told you I been watching things. I don't think you're doing so good.'

'Is that right?'

'Nobody's scared of you. They don't even know if you're serious.'

'Now you're a labor expert,' Mora said. 'The last I heard you were working in the laundry at Folsom.'

'Five years and three months.'

'How long you been out?'

'Little over a year.'

'You went back to East Los Angeles?'

'San Fernando.'

'That was it,' Mora said. 'And organized another Pachuco gang.'

'A self-defense group. You heard about it, uh?'

'I read something in *La Raza*. What do you call it? The brown something –'

'The Brown Hand.'

Mora nodded. '*Mano Castano*. Ex-cons teaching kids how to fight cops.'

'How to defend against police brutality,' Chino said.

'That's right, intimidation, persecution and entrapment.' Mora's tone was mild, almost musing. 'It's been a while,' he said. 'I've forgotten some of the words.'

'How to avoid being shot in the back for resisting arrest,' Chino said. 'Hit him first. Take the lead-weighted club away from the man and lay it across his face. He taught us how to do it.'

'Now you want to teach farm workers.'

'They're not pissed off enough to do you any good.'

Mora shrugged. 'They know what they want.'

'Knowing and getting – listen, you want to bust this grower. All right, I'll show you how, not take so much time.'

'Why? I mean why do you want to help?'

'For the good of my soul, Father, what do you think?'

'I think we're wasting time,' Mora said. 'Let's drink our coffee and you can tell me what it was like in the pen.'

'I'd rather ask you something,' Chino said. He was at ease, sitting low in the wooden office chair. 'I want to know who says you got a better reason for being here than me? You the new hope of the poor people? Tell me, who says your way is the only way?'

'Experience,' Mora said. 'Six years organizing in Coachella and the grape fields while you were in prison. Another reason – you see this as busting a grower. I want him to recognize a labor union.'

'It's the same thing. You want to win, I want to win.'

'Why?'

'For *them* – for myself, the same reason anyone's here.'

'The cause,' Mora said. 'The movement, uh?'

'Whatever you like to call it.'

'You still carry a can opener?'

'That was a long time ago.'

'Thirty-three stitches across the guy's stomach,' Mora said. 'What do you use now, a gun?'

'I use what I have to. You use a bullhorn and put everybody to sleep.'

Maybe you do waste words, Mora was thinking. And maybe it was a waste of time talking. But Chino was here and he could not close his eyes and make him go away; so he said, 'There's only one way to win. On the picket line. We stand there with our signs until the man sees we mean it and he begins to reason with himself. He doesn't want trouble. He wants his melons picked and sold and make a profit. He doesn't want fights and arrests, and have to spend his time in court. He's a businessman. So finally he talks to us and we let him bitch about the lousy market and high costs and the risks he takes, we don't say much. He already knows what we want. And pretty soon, after some more bitching, he agrees to most of the demands and we settle. Then do you know what? He feels pretty good about it, generous, like he's done us a favor. We go back to work and everybody's happy.'

'That's it, uh?'

'The only way.'

'If he feels good, I don't see you won anything.'

'I know you don't,' Mora said, 'because you don't want to bargain with the man, you want to punish him, kick his teeth out and burn his fields – the East L.A. Pachuco out to teach the gringo a lesson. Do you know what you're doing? Using La Causa as an excuse. And when you're called on it, you say, "No, man, it's nothing personal. Man, we're avenging years of serfdom and oppression."'

'That's what I think, uh?'

Mora drew on his cigarette and stubbed it out. 'Do you know, I spend half my time reminding people this is not a half-assed revolution, or a club for kids in Che Guevara T-shirts. It's a farm labor strike, nothing else.'

'You say it,' Chino said. 'But underneath it's a Chicano fight. You know it as well as I do. If it wasn't Chicano you wouldn't be here.'

Mora said quietly, 'We move a step at a time, put one foot in front of the other. First we get them a pay raise. Right now we have a chance of winning a strike, but not a riot. That's why we can't have violence.'

'They get rough, then what? Start swinging clubs?'

'We don't have a choice,' Mora said. 'Once we commit ourselves to a strike we have to do it legally. If they hit us, we cover our heads. No matter what they do we have to fight it legally or take it until they get tired and stop.'

'It's going to happen,' Chino said. 'First they try and scare you off, break a guy's leg. Next they get out the guns, scare hell out of your people.'

'They're showing the right signs,' Mora said. 'You were there today.'

'I mean when it gets rough,' Chino said. 'Shit, they don't even know yet it's going to be a war. You haven't told them what's going to happen, have you?'

'It doesn't have to happen.'

'But it will, because the grower and the cops don't have to put up with you.'

'Chino, I have to pick up Mrs Varrera at the hospital and I have to call a bondsman and do a few other things before I ever get to bed. You understand?'

'Still carrying the whole load,' Chino said. His eyes raised to the crucifix on the wall. 'You still pray?'

'I pray,' Mora said.

'So you still got enough priest left in you to believe God gives a shit who wins and it'll be you because you're on the side of right.'

'You don't have to be a priest,' Mora said, 'to have faith and hope.'

'Hope your people don't run. That's all you got to hope for. But when they do, or when there's some blood on the ground, then you'll see you're not the last hope of the poor people.'

'I'm a labor organizer,' Mora said, 'and maybe not a very good one. I know that. This is the first strike I've planned on my own and that I'm solely responsible for. So we'll have to wait and see whether I should stay in the business or not.'

'Just a labor organizer.' Chino nodded, sitting up and putting his hands on the edge of the desk. 'Maybe. But do you know what I think, Father? I think you're giving me a bunch of bullshit. I think the only reason you're here, you want to see your name in the paper again.'

'Chino, I'm tired. All right?'

'You don't want to talk about it.'

'There are things I have to do. I told you.'

'Some other time,' Chino said. 'I'll be around.'

When Chino had gone Mora sat at the desk and smoked a cigarette, and then another one, before he left to pick up Mrs Varrera at the hospital.

27.

Bud Davis took a six-pack of Lone Star with him to the Whataburger place. He sat there surrounded by brightly-lit tile and chrome and people he didn't know hunched over tables and put away a double Whataburger with everything on it, an order of fries and two of the beers. He sat by himself, staring at the highway through a wall of glass and seeing his own reflection superimposed on the cars that lined up for the stoplight – everybody going some place – and when the cars moved on he could make out the packing sheds and docks that were along the tracks on the other side of the road – dark and deserted-looking in the early evening dusk. He said to himself, What the fuck are you doin' here?

He walked north on Main Street carrying the four Lone Stars, taking his time and looking in the store windows. Half the signs were in Spanish. Most of the people he heard were speaking Spanish. The feature at the Rialto movie theater was a Spanish-language picture made in Mexico. He kept walking and after six blocks there were no more street lights and the road turned to blacktop.

Out in the darkness to the left, beyond an irrigation ditch and a mesquite thicket, was Gloria, where most of the field workers lived. It was called a *colonia*, though he didn't know why: a few yellowed-looking lights off there in the darkness and the sound of a dog barking. In the daylight Gloria was a scattered line of shacks made of adobe and tin and scrap board, hardpacked yards littered with kids and thrown-away junk and maybe a washing machine and a gutted car body without wheels. In the back, in the weeds, were outhouses and a stagnant drainage ditch they called Gloria Creek. He'd been over there a couple of days ago in the stake truck when Larry Mendoza was looking for pickers and had got only an old woman and a couple of kids about twelve. They don't feel like working, Mendoza had said, they go to Padre Island fishing or hang around a cafe. Christ.

It was almost another mile to Stanzik's property line and the migrant camp where Bud Davis was living. The camp had been built ten years before, during the *bracero* days, when thousands of Mexican nationals were brought into the Valley each season to harvest the crops. Now the corrugated shacks and the partitioned rooms in weathered one-story barracks were rented for a dollar a day to migrant families and strays like Bud Davis who came for a short time and moved on.

They didn't do much in the evening, the people who lived here. Some of them went to town and got drunk and Bud Davis wouldn't see them until morning. Some of the women did their laundry in the evening, in the washhouse where there were two cold water taps. Someone was always at the latrine, going in or going off in the bushes if the can was in use. There were kids all over the place, shrill voices from time to time in the darkness.

Picket Line

There were a few girls his age, but they were dogs, fat dumb-looking girls he'd have to be pretty hard up to mess with. He didn't know where Clinton Taylor went at night. Maybe there was a colored cafe in town or he went to one of the Mexican joints on the highway. Most of the people sat outside. He could see them in the light that showed in the open doorways. They'd sit there for hours and he'd hear the Spanish words and sometime their laughter and not ever know what they were talking about. Usually there would be a radio playing somewhere, but most of the sounds at night were Spanish and there was always a smell of wood smoke.

There were a couple of men on the steps of the barracks where his room was, smoking cigarettes, and they nodded when he sat down with them. After a silence one of them said, 'How you like work in the field?' Bud Davis said, 'Fine. I kind a like it, being outside. It's hard on the back though. I suppose till you get used to it.' They grinned and nodded again, but didn't say anything else. After a little while he went inside.

He'd brought a sleeping bag, which was a good move, since the company didn't provide bedding or blankets; but it was too hot to get inside the thing. He used it as a mattress, spread open on the cot. He undressed down to his undershorts and had another beer before it got too warm. Sitting there thinking, he decided that even if there was something to do at night, he'd be too tired to do it.

The sound of a car engine woke him up: a big-bore high-compression engine with a rough idle. He listened to it and then heard voices speaking in English and laughter: young male voices. He lay quietly.

One of the voices said, 'Come on, man, where're the girls? We're lookin' for some ass . . . Tell 'em we'll pay 'em. Two bucks an hour. Make more'n they do in the field.' And laughter again. And another voice saying, 'Come on, he don't know anybody.' And the first voice saying, 'Man, we used to get it here all the time.' The heavy rumble of the engine continued, though there were no more voices. Finally the engine sound rose to a howl and the car accelerated out of the closeness of the frame buildings.

Bud Davis lay in the darkness with his eyes open, listening to the car in the distance and counting the gear shifts. When it was quiet again he said to himself, Man, really, what the fuck are you doin' here?

It was the next day that he walked out of the field.

Chick Killer

Karen Sisco was telling her dad, 'This guy wearing cowboy boots walks in the bar . . .'

Her dad said, 'I've heard it.'

'I'm serious,' Karen said. 'Yesterday afternoon, my last day a federal marshal after six and a half years. In less than an hour I'll hand in my star.' She paused, watching her dad. 'And Bob Ray Harris, high on our "5 Most Wanted" list walks in the bar. O'Shea's on Clematis, up the street from the courthouse. I'm waiting for my supervisor. You met him, Milt Dancey, the one recruited me out of Florida Atlantic. Milt's coming up from Miami and called to say he was stuck in traffic, 95 bumper to bumper. He'd be in West Palm in about an hour. Milt's idea, talk me out of leaving the marshals.'

'I can hear him,' her dad said. '"You want to work for your old man? Take over his investigations? Work your tail off getting the stuff on some poor guy in divorce court?" He says, "You should be ashamed of yourself."'

Karen and her dad sat in the Florida room of his home in Coral Gables, comfortable in wicker chairs done in green and red hibiscus patterns, their drinks on the bamboo cocktail table.

'I told Milt I'd made up my mind and wasn't going to change it. Three months on courtroom security's all I can take. Listen to lawyers nine to four. Take the defendant to a holding cell for baloney sandwiches. Milt said they were keeping an eye on me after socializing with the guy who broke out of Glades Correctional, Foley, the bank robber. I said, "*Socializ*ing, I shot him, didn't I, and brought him back?"'

'You did tell me you spent time with him,' her dad said, 'but not what you were doing.'

'I'm trying to tell you,' Karen said, 'about a wanted felon walking into O'Shea's, while I'm waiting for Milt. You know why I recognized him? I'm cleaning out my desk this afternoon and came across his wanted dodger, with mugshots. Bob Ray Harris, a forty-year-old white male born October the tenth.'

'Columbus Day,' her dad said.

'Wanted by Atlanta police for a double homicide. Two girls in a movie theatre. I remembered that one,' Karen said. 'A witness described the girls talking out loud and laughing. The guy sitting right behind them told the girls to shut up. They said something he didn't like. The witness said he watched the guy grab each one by the hair, pull their heads back as they started to scream, and cut their throats ear to ear with a switchblade.'

After a beat her dad said, 'He got up and left?'

'Once he'd wiped the blade. One of the girls had long blonde hair. That's what he used, her hair.'

'What was the movie?'

'*Bridesmaids.*' R-rated, the girls shouldn't of been there. The guy sitting behind Bob Ray almost asked him to remove his straw cowboy hat and was glad he didn't. Later, the girl at the candy counter – Bob Ray scared her to death asking for a box of popcorn – picked him out of mugshots as the guy in the hat. His dodger said he was wanted for stabbing his girlfriend. Also raping and stomping to death a sixteen-year-old girl in Orlando.'

Her dad said, 'Honey, you're working for Sisco Investigations, you won't run into anyone carries a switchblade.'

'I saw him come in O'Shea's and hold the door open to look

both ways down the street. Then walked up to the bar, his shirttail hanging out, and ordered a Diet Pepsi.'

'You were close enough to hear him?'

'I saw the can.'

'I was testing your power of observation.'

Sometimes her dad was funny. At seventy-six he'd been running his private investigations company in Miami for forty years; the only time inactive when his prostate was acting up and he got rid of it. He said, 'You wondered about his shirttail hanging out.'

'The knife in his back pocket,' Karen said. 'He began staring at me. Finally takes a swig of Pepsi and comes over to place the can on my table and lean over on his hands to tell me he was buying. "What would I like?"'

'You said no thanks or a double Early Times over crushed ice?'

'I did, but didn't see myself drinking it right away. This guy with a record of violence against women, pulled the chair out to sit down and there's my bag sitting on it. He picked it up and hefted it like he's gonna guess its weight and said, "What you got in there?" handing me the bag.'

'Your Sig Sauer,' her dad said, 'and a pair of cuffs.'

'Two,' Karen said, 'I always carry an extra pair. I laid the bag on my lap and worked the Velcro loose to slip my hand inside. I'm not gonna tell Bob Ray he's under arrest without a .38 pointing at him.'

'Well, since you're telling me about it,' her dad said, 'I believe this turned out in your favor.'

'Wasn't it in the paper?'

'Not the *Herald*. But you're sittin here, you must a put him on the floor and cuffed him.'

'You think he'd let me? This guy who killed at least four women we know of? He said, "I'm at the bar, I see you lookin' me over, like you're not sure you know me. We ever met somewheres?" I told him he looked like Brad Pitt with long hair coming out of his cowboy hat. He goes, "Yeah . . .?" grinning at me. He asked me how old I thought he was. I said, "Forty, this past October." He said, "How'd you know that?"'

Her dad said, 'You're givin' yourself away.'

'I'm a girl in a bar he'd like to take to a motel and beat the shit out of, after he rapes me. I asked him what his sign was. He said, "My sign?" I said, "You're a Libra, aren't you? Born in October?" I said I was a Libra too.'

'You're an Aries,' her dad said. 'Your mother knew all that stuff. I can see her with her tarot cards, doing a reading about me.'

Karen said, 'You want to hear what happened or keep interrupting? I said to Bob Ray, "When a Libra meets another Libra they can know things about each other." I made that up. I don't know anything about astrology. But this guy who stabs women, raped and stomped a girl to death, knows even less. I said, "You know what I've got in my handbag?"'

'You're callin' him,' her dad said.

'He's seated at the table now. Leans back and says, "Oh, different kinds of girl shit. The bag has some weight. You got your vibrator in there?"'

'I told him I carry extra batteries for a recorder I speak into doing inventories at Supermarkets. "Twenty-four number ten cans of apricot halves in heavy syrup." While I'm telling him what a wonderful job it is – you know I did it while I was at school – I slipped my left hand into the bag to take off the safety while I picked up the drink with my right hand.'

Her dad stared at her not saying a word. But then asked, 'Why'd he bring up his age? Wantin you to guess how old he was?'

'I suppose 'cause most girls, scared shitless, told him he looked, oh, real young, something he loved to hear. I can't think of another reason. The bag's still on my lap and I asked him, "You want to see my equipment?" He said, "Your equipment, huh," grinning at me. He said, "Like the different parts that make you a hot chick?"'

'You're bringin' him along,' her dad said, 'but where you goin' with it?'

'We're there,' Karen said. 'Time to make the move. I said to him, "What am I getting out of this deal?" He said, "Honey, you get *me*." Oh really? I said, "I hear you like to beat up girls." He lost his grin and tried frowning, hard, wanting to know where I got that idea. I'm holding the Sig in one hand, the double bourbon in the other and I'm tempted to raise the glass and take a sip. So I did, and placed the glass on the table. Now I wanted a cigarette, but I'd better tend to business first. I said, "Bob Ray, I'm placing you under federal arrest. Keep your hands in sight, flat on the table. You try to get up, I'll shoot you." Now he put on a bewildered look showing me the palms of his hands saying, "Honey, I'm sure not who you say I am. Bob Ray who?"'

'I said, "Bob Ray Harris. You win the prize for being my last take-down as a deputy US marshal. You give me a hard time, I'll take my hand out of the bag and show you what I've got."'

Her dad wasn't saying a word.

'The guy was shaking his head, telling me he wasn't who I said he was, trying to push the chair back. He leaned against the table, his hands going behind him to his back pockets saying, "Lemme get out some I.D." My bag, with my hand in it, was pointed between his legs. I see his hand come around with the knife, the blade snapping out of the hilt, while aiming my handbag at him under the table. I fired, put a hole in my bag that grooved his thigh and he howled. Three feet away he's trying to push to his feet to get at me, strike with the knife and I shot him again.'

Her dad sat there staring at his little girl.

'In the balls this time,' his little girl said, 'and put him out of business.'

They both picked up their drinks from the bamboo table, her dad saying, 'Your boss finally got there?'

'Milt arrived while they were hauling Bob Ray out on a gurney.'

'You talked to him?'

'Milt? Yes, I did.'

'He's taking you off court security, isn't he?'

'Yes, he is.'

'And you want to stay with the marshals.'

'If you don't mind,' Karen said.

Ice Man

The day Victor turned twenty he rode three bulls, big ones, a good 1800 pounds each – Cyclone, Spanish Fly and Bulldozer – rode all their bucks and twists, Victor's free hand waving the air until the buzzer honked at eight seconds for each ride, not one of the bulls able to throw him. He rolled off their rumps, stumbled, keeping his feet and walked to the gate not bothering to look at the bulls, see if they still wanted to kill him. He won Top Bull Rider, $4000 dollars, and a new saddle at the All-Indian National Rodeo in Palm Springs. It came to . . . Jesus, like $200 dollars a second. That afternoon Victorio Colorado, the name he went by in the program, was the man.

*

He left the rodeo grounds as Victor to celebrate with two Mojave boys, Nachee and Billy Cosa, brought along from Arizona when the boss, Kyle McCoy, moved his business to Indio, near Palm Springs. The Mojave boys handled Kyle's fighting bulls, bringing them from the pens to the chute where Victor, a Mimbreño Apache, would slip aboard from the fence, wrap his hand in the bull rope tight as he could get it, and believe he was ready to ride. He'd take a breath, say, 'Let me out of here,' and the gate would swing open and a ton of pissed-off bull would come flying out.

'His mind made up,' he told the Mojave boys at Mi Nidito

in Palm Springs, 'to kill anybody's on his back. See, he behaves in the chute. What he's doing, he's saving his dirty tricks till he has room to buck you off and stomp you, kick out your teeth.'

They were at a table on the bar side of the place, Mi Nidito, a good one, some Agua Caliente Indians here after the rodeo. Victor was telling stories his Mojave buddies had heard, but they were happy, Victor was buying the tequila shooters and beers. Now he was telling them what he'd learned about bulls working for Kyle McCoy since he was a kid: how to ride the bucks tight, feel what the bull was about to do next. 'I ask Kyle, What's that mean? Feel what he's gonna do? I'm asking him how to ride a bull twenty times bigger than me. Kyle goes, "You become one with the bull or land on your ass." I had to figure out for myself what he meant. Two years in a row Kyle McCoy's world's best bull rider, twenty-four, twenty-five years old. Five years later he's world champion again and said, that's it, quit before he ever landed on his head. Kyle wore his range hat, never put on that helmet they offer you now. Quit in pretty good shape and moved to Indio to raise his bulls.'

'All killers,' Nachee said.

'But he started with heifers,' Victor said. 'You approach a mean heifer out on the graze? She gives you a dirty look and chases you the hell off.'

Victor saw Nachee and Billy Cosa looking toward the entrance and turned his head to see a Riverside County deputy talking to the manager. Some more law was outside. They'd go around to the kitchen and check on Mexicans without any papers. Victor saw the Riverside deputy look his way. No, he was looking at the white guy at the next table, the guy wearing a straw Stetson he'd fool with, raising the curled brim and setting it close on his eyes again. Never changed his expression. He had size, but looked ten years past herding cows. It was the man's US Government jacket told Victor he was none of their business. Victor said to his buddies:

'What Kyle did, he'd look for heifers were always pissed off and started with two of the meanest girls he could find. He named one Stormy, after a stripper he'd see he went to New Orleans, and the other one Julie, after the movie star was his girlfriend on and off, everybody thinking they'd get married till she walked out on him. Kyle was spending more time getting his heifers laid than whatever he was doing with Julie Reyes.'

'He was crazy,' Billy Cosa said. 'Julie Reyes is the coolest chick I ever saw in my life. She look at you with her dark eyes has lights in them . . .? Man, I forget what I'm saying to her.'

Victor said he heard Julie was in Hollywood making vampire movies. 'And Kyle's in the bull-humping business. Kyle's making more money than he ever did rodeoin' and I guess Julie's a movie actress.'

'Vampire flicks,' Nachee said. 'I see her last one, I come out of the show after, Kyle McCoy's there lighting up. I smoke one with him, ask him how he like the flick. He say he don't care for her being a vampire. A week later he sole Julie, asking a hundred grand and got close to it.'

'He sole the girl name Julie,' Billy Cosa said, 'or the heifer?'

Nachee raised one hand to give Billy a lazy high-five.

The white dude in the cowboy hat, still watching them, was laughing out loud.

Victor looked over to see him grinning now, the guy telling them, 'I'd say the boy's in trouble, he don't know a woman from a cow. Else he's had too much firewater.'

By this time Victor believed he and the Mojave boys had each put down four shots of tequila, toasting his rides, and a few Dos Equis for chasers. No matter, he was celebrating with his NDN brothers and would tell this nitwit Billy was kidding. But then he was thinking, Why you want to explain it to him?

'Cause he wears a US Government jacket? Now the white guy was getting up from the table, and Victor looked at his buddies and shook his head once, side to side and said, 'Don't fuck with him,' though he believed he probably would.

This guy in the cowboy hat was standing now, watching a girl coming from the bar with a drink in her hand. She walked up to the nitwit saying, 'The bartender finally got the Stoli Doli right.'

She stood with the white dude listening to him talking to her, nodding his cowboy hat at the three boys.

The girl's shirt was open two buttons, and her hair was mussed. The US Government white dude leaned close to tell her – maybe, Victor thought – what he was going to do next. The girl seemed to listen but without much interest. Now she was taking a pack of cigarettes from her shirt pocket, got one out but didn't light it, waiting for the white guy.

He stood there a moment adjusting his hat, setting it close on his eyes, the curved brim pointing at Victor. Now he used both hands to pop the snaps on his US Government jacket. He held it open so they could read the words reversed in white on the dark T-shirt. It said in capital letters:

ICE MAN

He said, 'Fellas, you happen to know what I.C.E. stands for?'

Victor could tell him it meant Immigration and Customs Enforcement, you turkey, but said, 'Does it mean you deliver ice to places like this one for drinks, maybe shrimp cocktails? I understand it's what icemen do, but I don't think I know any.'

'What I deliver,' the Ice Man said, 'I take illegal aliens to prison. People speaking foreign tongues and think obeying the law's a bunch of shit, refuse to follow the goddamn law of the land. I heard you saying you work for Kyle McCoy, but I don't recall seeing you since Kyle moved out here. I suppose 'cause you people, same as the colored, all look pretty much the same. You know what white people in olden times use to call Indins? Goddamn red n—.'

Victor said, 'You know what Apaches still call white people? "Los Goddamies," because many of you cannot talk without swearing. You use God's name even when you don't have a reason to. Maybe you agree with me, maybe you don't. But you said people who speak in foreign tongues refuse to follow the goddamn laws of the land. You saying all of us should speak only English?'

This Ice Man took time to stare at Victor. He said, 'They teach you that at Indin school? I hope you aren't getting smart with me. I see you drinkin' . . . Can you show me you're old enough by law?'

Victor said, 'This is what it's about, my age?'

'You show me you're old enough,' the Ice Man said, 'I'll let you step outside and arrest you for being shit-faced drunk.'

'You kidding me?'

'Drunk and disorderly, arguing with me.'

Victor said, 'You go to all this trouble –'

Nachee said, 'Because we NDN, we must be drunk.'

'The three of you actin' up,' the Ice Man said. 'I been watchin' you since you come in.'

'Man,' Nachee said, 'Victor rode three bulls today. We drinking to his honor.'

'What'd he win,' the Ice Man said, 'trading beads?'

'Four thousand dollars, man, and a saddle.'

Victor took the roll of bills from his shirt pocket and laid the wad on the table.

The Ice Man, looking at the money, raised his hat and set it on his head again saying, 'The bulls buck any, or they too old? I can cite you now for tryin' to bribe an officer of the law.'

Victor said, 'I'm not offering you anything.'

'You're mouthin' off, arguing with me. Give me your names and we'll get her done.'

Victor said, 'My Mimbreño Apache name is Deer with Horns Running Through the Woods Being Chased by a White Dude Wearing a Cowboy Hat.'

Nachee said, 'You know Agua Calientes operate the casinos? They get to watch white men become drunk and lose all their money.'

'Keep talking,' the Ice Man said.

Nachee said, 'You know how NDNs know it's safe to go fishing in the winter? When all the white guys quit falling through the fucking ice.'

This time the Ice Man only stared, no expression on his face.

'I was in a bar,' Nachee said, 'where a white man with a cigar was blowing smoke rings, nine or ten of them hanging in the air. I look at the rings and said to him, "One more remark like that, I'll bust you in the mouth."'

The Ice Man said, 'I was at a Indin wedding on the rez one time. The flower girls were all the bride's kids, her bastards. You hear that one? Or, how do you tell a rich Indin from a poor one? The rich Indin has two cars up on blocks.' He waited a moment and said, 'We're through here,' picked up his cell phone and said, 'Wesley, I might need a hand.'

What was going on? Nachee never carried ID working bulls. Victor didn't either. They both believed if you know who you are, what do you need ID for? You want to tell somebody your name, tell him. You don't want to, don't.

The only question Nachee thought of: why did Kyle McCoy move his bull ranch from Arizona to Indio, California? The only reason he could think of: now that Kyle's bulls were making him rich, he had time for Julie Reyes in Hollywood making movies. He hoped so. Nachee was dying to see her again.

He saw deputies in their serious hats coming through the restaurant from the kitchen, four white guys who looked like they meant business, serious, minds made up, and Nachee thought of a grandfather now from the other time, more than a hundred years ago, Nachitay sitting in Mi Nidito with Victor's grandfather from the same time, Victorio. Sometimes Nachee talked to Victor about those guys living the way they chose to. You hungry? Run off a mule, cut steaks and cook them over a fire. Before General Crook came along on his mule, the one Nachee's grandfather from that other time was dying to eat. Bring them all here to sit with their rifles, Victorio, Cochise, Geronimo . . . those guys doing whatever they wanted. They never carried ID but every horse soldier in the Arizona Territory knew who they were. Now the deputies were coming and Nachee, smiling as they reached the table, said:

'What can I do for you boys?'

One of the deputies banged his head down on the table, held him while they cuffed his hands behind his back.

'All three,' the Ice Man said, 'I'm placing these boys under federal arrest.'

The deputy he'd spoken to on the phone, Wesley, said, 'What have you thought of to charge 'em with?'

'Mouthin' off,' the Ice Man said, stepping over to pick up the fold of hundred-dollar bills Victor had dropped on the table. They had Victor bent over now handcuffing him. Victor straining to look at the Ice Man riffling through his bills.

'You know that's rodeo money I won today.'

'How much you have left?'

'Four thousand. I haven't spent none.'

'We'll catalogue it, pay your fines, your upkeep, you get your release I'll give you what's left,' the Ice Man said. 'How's that set with you?'

*

Celeste, the girl sipping a Stoli Doli earlier, was outside now having a cigarette.

She said to the Ice Man, 'You finished holding up the law?'

'They're in detention till I say let 'em out.'

'The only reason being they're Indians?'

The Ice Man's name was Darryl Harris.

He said, 'What's wrong with that?'